Scary Sto
Ten Yea

Helen Paiba is known as one of the most committed, knowledgeable and acclaimed children's booksellers in Britain. For more than twenty years she owned and ran the Children's Bookshop in Muswell Hill, London, which under her guidance gained a superb reputation for its range of children's books and for the advice available to its customers.

Helen was involved with the Booksellers Association for many years and served on both its Children's Bookselling Group and the Trade Practices Committee. In 1995 she was given honorary life membership of the Booksellers Association of Great Britain and Ireland in recognition of her outstanding services to the association and to the book trade. In the same year the Children's Book Circle (sponsored by Books for Children) honoured her with the Eleanor Farjeon Award, given for distinguished service to the world of children's books.

She retired in 1995 and now lives in London.

Titles available in this series

Funny Stories for Five Year Olds
Magical Stories for Five Year Olds
Animal Stories for Five Year Olds

Funny Stories for Six Year Olds
Magical Stories for Six Year Olds
Animal Stories for Six Year Olds

Funny Stories for Seven Year Olds
Scary Stories for Seven Year Olds
Animal Stories for Seven Year Olds

Funny Stories for Eight Year Olds
Scary Stories for Eight Year Olds
Animal Stories for Eight Year Olds

Funny Stories for Nine Year Olds
Scary Stories for Nine Year Olds
Animal Stories for Nine Year Olds

Funny Stories for Ten Year Olds
Scary Stories for Ten Year Olds
Animal Stories for Ten Year Olds

Coming soon

Adventure Stories for Five Year Olds
Adventure Stories for Six Year Olds
Adventure Stories for Seven Year Olds
Adventure Stories for Eight Year Olds
Adventure Stories for Nine Year Olds
Adventure Stories for Ten Year Olds

Scary

STORIES

for Ten Year Olds

COMPILED BY HELEN PAIBA

ILLUSTRATED BY DAVID FRANKLAND

MACMILLAN
CHILDREN'S BOOKS

First published 2000 by Macmillan Children's Books
a division of Macmillan Publishers Limited
25 Eccleston Place, London SW1W 9NF
Basingstoke and Oxford
www.macmillan.co.uk

Associated companies throughout the world

ISBN 0 330 39126 7

3 5 7 9 8 6 4 2

A CIP catalogue record for this book is available
from the British Library.

Typeset by SX Composing DTP, Rayleigh, Essex
Printed and bound in Great Britain by
Mackays of Chatham plc, Kent

Contents

Mayday!

Redvers Brandling

Captain Ian Sercombe was frightened. He rested a broad forefinger on the control column of the Boeing 747 and eased back in his seat. Glancing out of the cabin windows at the sixty metres of his giant machine's wingspan he tried to calm himself with thoughts of its size and detail . . . as high as a six-storey building, over two hundred kilometres of wiring, four million parts, space for more than four hundred passengers . . .

"Decent night, Skip."

First Officer Les Bright's voice cut in on Ian's thoughts. The two men had completed the pre take-off check and were sitting on the flight deck. Outside a huge moon hung in the hot tropical night sky which pressed down on Singapore's Changi Airport.

Les Bright was talking to the control tower when Cabin Service Director Edwina Reeves came into the flight deck area.

1

"Two hundred and sixty passengers and thirteen cabin crew all safely on board, Captain. Cabin secure."

"Thanks, Edwina," replied Ian. "We should be off very soon."

Minutes later the huge aircraft began to roll away from its stand at the airport. The time was 8.04pm and the journey to Perth, Australia had begun.

Within an hour all was routine on the flight deck. The Jumbo was cruising at Flight Level 370, about seven miles above sea level. Speed was 510 knots and the course was 160° magnetic as the plane, under the automatic pilot, headed south over Indonesia.

"Weather ahead looks good," commented First Officer Bright, nodding at the weather radar screen which promised three hundred miles of smooth flying ahead.

"Hmmm," agreed Ian.

He had been studying the weather radar with unusual intensity – just as he had all the other complex instruments in the cabin. But the fear wouldn't go away. It wasn't nervousness . . . or apprehension . . . Ian Sercombe was frightened. He could only ever remember feeling like this once before, and that had been the dreadful day of the accident . . .

Ian and his lifelong friend Mike Payne had been

crewing together on a flight back from New York. Leaving the airport in Ian's car, they were accelerating on the M25 when a tyre burst. In the crash which followed Ian had been unhurt, but Mike was killed instantly. Just before the tyre went Ian had felt this unreasoning fear. Afterwards he could never quite rid himself of guilt for Mike's death. He'd been blameless perhaps – he'd checked the tyres just a couple of days previously – but how could Mike know that? Once again he thought of Mike's bluff, smiling Irish face, grinning as always and clapping those gloved hands together. Always been a joke between them that – the only pilot who never flew without wearing fine kid gloves.

Ian's thoughts were brought back to the present as First Officer Bright made a routine position report.

"Jakarta Control, Moonlight Seven over Halim at 20.44."

Then it started.

"Unusual activity on weather radar, Captain."

"I see it, Les."

"Just come up – doesn't look good."

"Could be some turbulence in that. Switch on the 'Fasten Seat Belts' sign."

The two pilots tightened their own seat belts. Behind them in the crowded cabins, passengers grumbled as they had to interrupt their evening meal to fasten their seat belts. Smiling stewardesses assured them there was no problem.

"Engine failure – Four!"

The flight engineer's terse voice cut the flight deck silence.

"Fire action Four," responded Ian simultaneously.

Together Les Bright and Engineer Officer Mary Chalmers shut off the fuel lever to Four and pulled the fire handle. There was no fire in the engine and Ian felt an easing of his tension.

No pilot likes an engine failure, but the giant Jumbo could manage well enough on the three that were left.

"Engine failure Two."

Mary Chalmers' voice was more urgent this time, but as she and Les Bright moved to another emergency procedure she suddenly gasped breathlessly.

"One's gone . . . and Three!"

Seven miles high with two hundred and seventy-three people on board, the Boeing was now without power. Ian knew that the huge plane could only glide – and downwards.

"Mayday, Mayday, Mayday!" First Officer Bright's voice barked into the emergency radio frequency. "Moonlight Seven calling. Complete failure on all engines. Now descending through Flight Level 360."

Ian's hands and mind were now working with

automatic speed. He again checked the fuel and electrical systems. Emergency restarting procedures failed to have any effect. Quickly he calculated their terrible position. The plane was dropping at about two hundred feet per minute . . . which meant that in twenty-three minutes' time . . .

"You two," said Ian quietly to the First Officer and Flight Engineer. "I'm going to need all the help I can get later on, but there could be problems back there with the passengers now – especially as we're obviously going down. Go back – help out – and get back here as soon as you can."

Bright and Mary Chalmers climbed out of their seats, slamming the door to the flight deck behind them as they went to try and reassure the terrified passengers.

Ian was now alone on the flight deck.

"Problems," he muttered aloud. "Crash landing in the sea so keep the wheels up, lights are going to fail because there's no generated power from the engines, standby power from the batteries won't last long . . ."

The closing of the flight deck door interrupted Ian's monologue.

"All right back there?" he asked, as the First Officer climbed back into his seat. He was just able to make out his fellow pilot's quick nod in the rapidly dimming light on the flight deck.

"It's too risky to try and get over those mountains now," said Ian. "What do you think?"

"Go for the sea," was the reply, in a strangely muffled tone.

Ian's arms were aching from holding the lurching and buffeting aircraft, but he was surprised when the First Officer leaned over and laid a hand on his shoulder. It seemed to have both a calming and strengthening effect.

"I'll take her for a while."

The giant plane continued to drop. At 14,000 feet the emergency oxygen masks had dropped from the

roof for passengers' use. Now the rapidly dropping height was down to 13,000 feet.

"I'll save myself for the landing," muttered Ian, watching his co-pilot in admiration. In the dim light the First Officer was a relaxed figure, almost caressing the jerking control column. His touch seemed to have calmed the aircraft too. Its descent seemed smoother, almost gentle even.

13,000.

12,000.

11,000.

"Ian."

The captain was startled by the unexpected use of his Christian name by the First Officer.

"Volcanic dust and jet engines don't mix. I think we should make another re-light attempt on the engines now."

Still feeling calm, even relaxed considering the terrible situation they were in, Ian began the engine restarting drill yet again.

"Switch on igniters . . . open fuel valves . . ."

As suddenly as it had failed, Engine Four sprang back into life.

"We've got a chance!" cried Ian.

"Go for the rest," was the quiet reply.

Expertly, Ian's hands repeated the procedure. There was a lengthy pause then . . . Bingo! Number

Three fired ... then One ... and then Two.

"We'll make it after all," sighed Ian, once again taking a firm grip of the controls.

"Les – get on to Jakarta Control and tell them what's happening ... Les ..."

To his astonishment, when Ian looked to his right only the gentle swaying control column came into view. The First Officer had gone. It was then that the captain heard the crash of the axe breaking through the door to the flight deck.

Engineer Chalmers was the first one through the shattered door.

"Fantastic, Skipper, fantastic – how did you do it?"

"Incredible!"

This was Les Bright's voice.

"The flight deck door jammed and we've been stuck out there for five minutes wondering how on earth you were getting on – and now this! You're a marvel, Skipper."

Ian glanced up at the animated face of his First Officer in the brightening light of the flight deck.

"But ..."

The rest of the words died on his lips. A feeling of inexplicable gratitude and calm swept over him. He remembered the confident, sure figure who had so recently sat in the co-pilot's seat. He now remembered too that just before the lights had reached their dimmest he had noticed that the hands holding the controls were wearing a pair of fine kid gloves.

"Get on to Jakarta," Ian said quietly. "Tell them we're coming in."

The Mirror

Ann Carroll

For a few months when I was thirteen Caroline was my best friend. I still miss her and wish we could talk and laugh again, that we could've gone through college together. But of course that was never possible.

Ten years ago our family moved to Dublin. Mom and Dad wanted to take their time buying a home, so they rented an old furnished house in Roebuck, Clonskeagh. The first time I saw it was when we moved in that September afternoon. We stood in the front garden under the chestnut tree surveying the house. It had a basement, steps leading up to the front door and the date "1887" etched into the warm stone of the lintel.

"I bags the basement, Sarah," my brother Tom said. It had a separate entrance. Tom was sixteen and this was the closest he would get for quite a while to having his own pad.

"It's for both of you—" Mom began firmly.

"He can have it," I said, staring up at the second floor window, "if I can have that room." I pointed and Mom glanced up.

"You haven't even seen it, but, yes, you can have it."

I looked again at the perfectly proportioned window and caught my breath. The afternoon sun glittered on the pane and in the dazzling light I saw a face. Shading my eyes I stared. The pale features of a girl stared back.

"Mom, Dad! Can you see anyone at the window?" As I watched, the face faded.

Dad shook his head and Mom said, "It's just the branches of the tree reflected in the glass."

Tom laughed and put on a spooky voice. "Woooh! It's the ghost of 1887 and it's haunting your bedroom!" He could be a terrible pain.

"Well," I said calmly, "I'd better take one of the basement rooms so." Of course I'd no intention of doing this. Having my own personal ghost was far more exciting than watching the basement become a bomb site under Tom's tenancy. But it was satisfying to see his face drop.

"I was only kidding," he said. "There's no ghost!"

"It'd be too scary to sleep up there now after what you said."

Mom and Dad were climbing the steps to the door.

"I'll give you a fiver, Sarah!" He was urgent.

I calculated. "Do you have a tenner?"

His eyes narrowed. "No I don't, Greedy Guts!"

"Too bad. Anyway I'm looking forward to the basement. I can bring in all the new friends I make at—" Tom dug deeply into the pocket of his jeans and handed me a tenner. "Oh thank you, Tom!" I took the money and sauntered up the steps.

The bedroom was old-fashioned but nice. Dark red and gold wallpaper, velvety to the touch. Rugs on the polished wooden floor, a fireplace in the centre of one wall and a wardrobe in the corner painted with a border of fading flowers. A desk and chair at the window and a high single bed standing against the opposite wall.

A breeze rustled through the chestnut tree and a branch tapped on the window, extending a welcome. The room was warm, gilded in the September sunlight and I loved it. I stood on the chair and put my unpacked case away on the top shelf of the wardrobe. That was when I saw the doll. She was at the back of the shelf and the case tipped her forward. Her blue eyes blazed in a shaft of sunlight.

Carefully I lifted her out and set her on the desk. A fine lawn dress and three layers of petticoats covered the cloth body. The silver and gold embroidery on the frock was grimy with dust and age and the auburn hair was dull. Her hands and feet were tiny, their perfect creamy porcelain matched her face. She was beautiful. Her mouth curved in a smile, her eyes steady, not hard as glass should be, but soft and luminous. I knew she belonged to the girl I had seen at the window.

Two weeks later I started at the convent school on the hill. It was impossible to make friends. My accent was different and the size of the building bewildered me. I was like a stranger in a foreign land, an outsider. The country village I'd come from was quiet, its school small and the pace of life slow. Here

there were nearly a thousand students and whenever a bell rang the corridors swarmed with screeching girls and cross teachers. The place bristled with rules and impatience. Most of the first week I was lost, getting the head snapped off me for coming late to lessons, much to my classmates' amusement. I longed for the easy going ways of my village school, missing my old friends.

The loneliness would have been unbearable without the haven of my room. Throughout that September and October the days were mellow and warm, my room peaceful and silent. As soon as possible after school I retreated there. I did not even play my Walkman and hated it when faint sounds of Tom's music came from the basement.

At first Mom wondered why I wanted to spend all my time there.

"Homework," I said. "Projects to do. Essays to write."

"It must be a great school," she said faintly. "You used to say homework was a horrible disease."

"That was when I was immature," I said. "Now I know how important it is."

She felt my forehead. "Are you sure you're not sick, Sarah?"

I looked wounded and she went off muttering.

Of course she came up to my room a few times after

that. Always the books were open and I managed to look studious.

But mostly I was dreaming. I lay on the bed and stared across the room at the doll. If I focused steadily, then eventually, in the gathering twilight, a girl's face took shape, pale and sad. She was about my age, a bit old for the doll, which must have been a childhood gift, too precious for throwing out.

I never spoke, sure that the sound of my voice would shatter her image. The trance was broken only by someone calling from below, or the sound of Mom's footsteps on the stairs which made me dive for the chair and the books.

Maybe I would have come to believe what I saw was a figment of my imagination. Certainly I couldn't have gone on for ever staring at her silent features. The restless energy of adolescence would have asserted itself and soon enough I'd have gone on my way, the face at the window fading from memory.

Instead, at Halloween, Tom found the mirror, oval with a gilt frame.

"It was hidden behind a press in the basement," he said. "Whoever put it there didn't want it and I don't either. You can't see yourself properly in it. It's dim, so I thought, hey, it'll suit Sarah!"

The mirror was about three foot high and I

thought its soft reflection was lovely.

"That was meant to be a joke," Tom said. "Not a great joke, I admit, but it was worth a smile."

I said nothing, trying to work out the writing on the back of the frame. He sighed.

"Come on. I'll help you put it up."

In my room he noticed something I'd completely missed. "Look at this, Sarah! There's an oval outline on the wall. I bet the mirror belongs to this room. There's even a kind of hook here."

"It probably goes into this groove." I showed him the indentation above the inscription.

"Can you make out the writing, Tom?"

He peered at the words, rubbing the dust off with his sleeve. "It's a name," he said. "Caroline . . . Caroline Esther O'Connor . . . Age: thirteen . . . 1900. She was born in 1887, Sarah, the year the house was built!"

The mirror fitted snugly on the wall, but I had no time to study it because Dad's sister, Aunt Rita, was coming to visit and I had to play the dutiful niece.

Generally I hated this. It meant being polite while Aunt Rita fussed over me for ten minutes and ignored me for the rest of the evening. It could be so boring listening to the adults. Mostly they went on and on about politics and religion and people they knew and I hadn't a clue about. I usually switched off, but that night Aunt Rita said something to jolt me right out of my own world.

"You know, Sam," she told my dad, "our mother's family, the O'Connors, used to live in this area. At the beginning of the century, I think. She mentioned a stone house in Roebuck once, with the date over the door. Perhaps it was this very house!"

Of course it was, you fool! I wanted to scream with excitement. Caroline Esther O'Connor lived here when she was my age. Perhaps she was my great great grandmother or aunt . . .

For a moment I thought of telling them about the mirror and caught Tom's questioning glance. But I shook my head. Aunt Rita would start braying over it. Dad would want its value assessed immediately and Mom would want to hang it somewhere more public, like the hall, where she could show it off as a piece of family history.

"Why did the O'Connors move away from Dublin?" Dad asked.

"Some family tragedy," Aunt Rita said. "And the father inherited a farm in West Cork. The way Mother told it, the family were glad to move away, though she wasn't at all clear on the details."

Later in my room I stood in front of the mirror. The old glass glimmered in the lamplight as I called her name, "Caroline . . . Caroline . . ."

The light went out and in the darkness someone brushed against me. My breathing stopped and I froze. There was a rustle and a small cough before the room brightened again. I closed my eyes.

"Sarah." Her voice was as normal as my own. Then looking at the mirror I saw her, the girl from the window, her hair the same burnished colour as my own, only much longer.

"Sarah," she said again and touched my arm.

I turned and smiled. "Hello, Caroline."

She was about my height, my build, my colouring and I thought, "This is exactly how I would have looked in 1900." Her dress was light blue, ankle

length, with a pattern of tiny flowers and over it she wore a darker blue pinafore, to match the colour of her slippers.

"I'm glad you found the mirror," she said. "It's been so lonely in this house. Now at last I have someone to talk to."

"Do you realize how alike we are?" I blurted. "Do you realize we're related?" Then I told her what Aunt Rita said about my grandmother's people. She was thoughtful.

"Maybe that's why you were able to call me back," she said, "because we have the same bloodline. That must be the reason." After a silence she went on. "There was another girl I tried to contact once. She was my age too. I wanted to reach her from the mirror. She could sense I was there, but she couldn't see me. She grew more and more afraid and one day she wrenched the mirror from the wall and took it away, leaving me stranded."

"But I could see you, Caroline, without the mirror."

"Could you?" she asked. "But not properly, very faintly, and not to speak to. Not like this."

We talked through the night, new friends, curious to know all about one another. She spoke as though 1900 were the present. "My older sister Eileen is married and lives in London. Then there's Richard. He's twenty. Father says he's far too wild. He wants to fight in the Boer war, but Father's sent him off to New York on family business and says that should keep him occupied. John is the youngest. He's nine and a dreadful nuisance. I wish *he* could go off to some war!"

In turn I told her about my old life and how I missed the village school and all my friends. I described Tom and his horrible music. "He's into Heavy Metal," I said, "and he loves Raves, though Mom hates him going 'cos she thinks everyone there is on Ecstasy and . . ." I stopped. Caroline was looking mystified.

"Is he somewhat astray?" she said. "Has he a delicate brain?"

Since there was nothing at all "delicate" about Tom, it was my turn to feel puzzled.

"I mean, Sarah, with his habit of raving and his ecstatic moods, the way he treats metals – would he be a poor lunatic?"

"Well . . . yeah . . . I suppose so. But it's nothing to worry about." There was obviously no point discussing Tom with her. He was beyond anyone's understanding, especially anyone born in the nineteenth century.

We talked till daylight penetrated the heavy

curtains and the lamp faded and Dad shouted at me to get up.

"Call for me again tonight," Caroline said and disappeared as I got ready for school.

And so, a pattern was established. Each night, after everyone had gone to bed and there was no danger of intrusion, I looked in the mirror and called her name. I never tired of hearing her stories.

"Father planted that chestnut tree the day I was born," she told me. "He says chestnut trees are possessed of beauty and long life and those are the gifts he wishes for me."

Caroline's eyes filled with tears and to distract her I asked, "Who gave you the doll?"

"Eileen sent it from London when I was nine. She's called Miranda."

Sometimes we played cards. She knew Snap and Twenty-Five and I taught her Mexican Sweat. Or we discussed books we'd both read, like *Jane Eyre* and *Wuthering Heights*. Sometimes we sat in silence, drawing or painting.

In spite of the long night hours I never felt tired in her company. We giggled a lot, but never argued. Our opinions were so alike, especially on books and brothers. And since she came from another time there was something magical about our friendship.

But often during the day I could not keep my eyes open and got into trouble for nodding off in class. At home Mom began to pass remarks on my increasing paleness and talked about tonics and how I shouldn't go mad altogether studying. "So much schoolwork couldn't be healthy," she said.

"You used to give out when I did none," I told her.

Wait till she saw the Christmas report. That'd show her exactly how well I'd studied!

On Christmas Eve I gave Caroline my painting of the chestnut tree. Her gift was a brilliant pen and ink drawing of her family. Her small brother, John, was the image of Dad in the photograph we had of him as a boy.

I started telling her Mom and Dad's news about the new house they'd bought and how we planned to move in the new year.

"But you can't move, Sarah. You can't leave me here!" She was very upset and I stared at her, appalled.

"Of course I won't leave you here," I said. "I'll bring you with me when I take the mirror."

"You can't bring me with you. I belong to this room, to this house. You must stay here, Sarah. Stay with me, in the mirror."

The thought horrified me and I drew back, frightened.

She was desperate. "Sarah, there will be no one to call me when you are gone."

Her loneliness was terrible.

"But why must you stay here?" I said. "What ties you to this room?"

For the first time she spoke of the past, admitting at last that for her there was no present and no future.

"Father's wish for me didn't come true. When I was thirteen, in December, I got scarlet fever and died in this room. I didn't want to go. One day, Eileen and Richard would come home to visit and I wanted to see them. Neither could I leave Mother and Father or even John. We'd been so happy here."

She sighed. "On Christmas Eve I was very ill. Mother left the room to get a fresh basin of water. I struggled out of bed and managed to reach the mirror, wanting to see how poorly I was. Looking in the glass I knew. Then I made my wish never to leave. I made it with all my heart." She frowned, unhappiness clouding her face. "I could see their sorrow when I was dead, and wanted to tell them that wasn't really me lying there, but their minds were numb with grief and they could not hear. No one came near the mirror. Afterwards, a neighbour arrived to tidy the room and I never saw my family again. None of them came in here. They forgot about me, Sarah. Then one day the house was empty. Only strangers lived here after that, until you came. Why did they leave me, Sarah, when I wanted so much to be with them?"

I pieced together what I knew from Aunt Rita. "They could not bear your death," I said, "that's why they never came in here. That's why they left. It was sorrow, not forgetfulness. They'd no idea you were still here. If they had, they would never have gone."

Slowly her expression changed. That immense sadness left her eyes and I said, "I think they've been waiting for you for a long time, Caroline. I reckon you should follow them. It's time to make another wish."

"Will you come with me, Sarah?"

I shook my head. "Even if I could, I wouldn't. I'd miss my own family too much. Surely you can understand . . ."

She nodded.

I watched her stand in front of the mirror and make her wish. Then she turned to me.

"Do you think we'll ever see each other again?"

Before I could answer, the curtains parted in the breeze and the morning light flooded the room, distracting my attention. When I looked back, she was gone.

*

I called her name a couple of times after that. There was no answer. Before we moved house a month later, I took the mirror down to the back yard and smashed the glass, then put the whole lot out for the binmen.

The Man Who Didn't Believe in Ghosts

Sorche Nic Leodhas

In a town not far from Edinburgh there was a house that was said to be haunted. It wasn't the sort of house you'd think would attract a ghost at all. It was only a two-storey cottage with a garret, and it was far too neat and pretty for ghosts to care much about. The outside walls of it were painted white and its casement windows had diamond-shaped panes to them. There was a climbing rose trained over the front door, and there was a flower garden before the house and a kitchen garden behind it, with a pear tree and an apple tree and a small green lawn. Who'd ever think that a ghost would choose to bide in a place like that? But folks did say it was haunted, all the same.

The house had belonged to an old lawyer with only one child, a daughter. Folk old enough to remember her still say that there never was another lass as bonny as her in the town. The old man loved her dearly but she died early. There was an old sad story told about her being in love with the son of an old laird who did not favour the match. The poor lad died of a fever while they were still courting, and not long after she died too – folk said of a broken heart.

After that the old man lived alone in the house, with a woman coming in each day to take care of it. There wasn't a word said about ghosts in the old man's time. He'd not have put up with it for a minute.

When the old lawyer died, there was nobody left that was kin to him but a second cousin several times removed. So to keep the property in the family, the old man left all he had to the cousin, including the house, of course.

The young man was grateful, but as he was not married, he had little use for a house. The lodgings he was living in suited him fine. So he put the renting of the house into an agent's hands. The rent money would make a nice little nest egg against the time when he decided he would like to get married. When that time came he'd want the house for himself.

It was the folks the agent found to live in the house that started all the talk about ghosts. At first they were very well pleased with the house, but as time passed they began to notice queer things were happening in it. Doors would open and close again, with nobody at all near them. When the young wife was dusting the spare bedroom, she heard drawers being pulled open and shut again behind her, but when she turned about to look, no one at all was there.

Things were lifted and put down again before the tenants' very eyes, but they couldn't see who was lifting them or putting them down. They came to have the feeling there was somebody always in the house with them. Of course, they tried to be sensible about it, but it gave them a terribly eerie feeling. As for getting a maid to stay, it couldn't be done! The maids all said that they felt that someone was always looking over their shoulders while they worked, and every time they set something down, it got itself moved to another place. They wouldn't take it upon themselves to say why, but they'd take whatever pay was coming to them, and go. And they did.

The end of the tenants' stay in the house came upon the day when the young wife came into the sitting-room to find her wee lad rolling his ball across the floor. Every time the ball reached the middle of the room it seemed to turn and roll itself back to him, as if someone who couldn't be seen were playing with him. But when he looked up at his mother and laughed and said, "Bonny lady!", 'twas more than she could bear. She caught him up in her arms and ran out of the door to one of her neighbours, and no one could persuade her to set foot in the house again. So her husband went to the agent and told him they were sorry, but the way things were, they'd have to give up the house.

The young man to whom the house had been left was a very matter-of-fact young fellow. He didn't believe in ghosts. He was quite put out because the story had got round that there were ghosts in the house. Of course, the young couple who had lived there couldn't be depended on not to talk about what had happened. It wouldn't have been according to

human nature for them to keep quiet about it. What made it awkward was that by this time the young man had found a lass he wanted to marry, but unfortunately she had heard the story. And she did believe in ghosts.

She said that she loved him dearly and would like very much to marry him. But she told him flatly that she could never, *never* bring herself to live in a haunted house.

Then the young man told her that he would go and live in the house himself, just to prove that there were no ghosts in it. Anyway, he didn't believe in ghosts. So he left his lodgings and moved in and got himself settled comfortably in his house.

Well, the doors did open and close of themselves, but that didn't daunt him. He just took them off their hinges and rehung them. They went on opening and closing just the same, but he said that was only because of a flaw in the walls.

He had to admit to himself that he heard drawers opening and closing, and latches of cupboards clicking shut. There was a tinkling in the china closet, too, as if someone were moving the cups and plates about. And once or twice he thought he heard water running in the scullery. But when he looked, every tap was shut off tight. Besides, he knew there was no one but himself in the house. So he said that old houses were always full of queer noises because of the foundations settling, and paid them no more heed.

Even when a book he had just closed and laid on the table opened itself again, and leaves turned over slowly as if someone were looking at them, he told himself that it was just a puff of wind from the window did it, although afterwards he remembered that the windows were closed at the time.

But still he didn't believe in ghosts.

So he went on living in the house and trying to persuade his sweetheart to marry him and come and live there with him. And, of course, to convince her that the house wasn't haunted at all. But he had no luck, for she wouldn't be persuaded.

Well, things went on in this unsatisfactory way until his summer holidays came round. He decided, now that he had the time for it, to do something he'd been meaning to do and never got round to. There were a lot of clothes in the attic that had belonged to the old lawyer and his daughter. It seemed sinful to leave them there to moulder away when some poor body'd be glad to have them. So what he was going to do was to pack them all up and send them to the Missionary Society where a good use would be found for them.

He went up to the garret and found some empty

boxes, and began to pack the clothes. They were all hanging in tall presses, ranged around the room. He packed the old lawyer's clothes first. There were a good many of them, suits and coats and boots and shoes, all of the best quality, to say nothing of a quantity of warm underclothing in boxes neatly stacked on the floors of the presses. When he had taken everything out and folded it neatly, he packed the boxes and set them out of his way, and turned to the press that held the dead lass's clothes.

When he opened the first press there was a sound uncommonly like a sigh. It gave him a start for a moment, but then he laughed and told himself that it was only the silk of garments brushing against each other in the breeze made by the opening door. He began to take them out, one by one, and to fold them and gently lay them in the box he'd set ready for them. It made him feel a little sad and sentimental to be handling the dresses that had been worn by the pretty young thing who had died so young and so long ago.

He'd laid away five or six of them when he came to one frock that seemed strangely heavy for the material of which it was made. It was a light, crisp cotton sprigged with flowers still bright in spite of the years it had hung in the press. He thought that a dress like that should have had almost no weight at all, so he looked it over curiously. Perhaps a brooch or a buckle was the answer?

Then he found a pocket set in the seam of the skirt, and in the pocket a small red book and a letter. It was a letter of the old style, with no envelope, and the dead girl's name and address on the outer folded sheet. He laid the dress aside and, taking his find to the low-set window, he sat down on the floor to read what he had found. He was not a man to read other people's letters and secrets, but something made him feel that it was right to do so now.

He read the letter first. It said:

My dear love:
Although they have not told me, I know that I am very ill. It may be that we shall not meet again in this world. If I should die I beg of you make them promise that when you, too, are dead we shall lie together side by side.

Your true love

The young man sat for a while, thinking of the letter, wondering how it had come to the lass, remembering that he had heard that the old laird was hard set against the match. Then he took up the little red book and opened it. The little book was a sort of day-by-day diary with the date printed at the top of each page. It had begun as a sort of

housekeeping journal. There was a lot in it about household affairs. There were records of sewing done, of jars of pickles and jams laid by, and about the house being turned out and cleaned from end to end, and such things. But through it all was the story of a young girl's heart. She told about meeting the laird's son, where they first met and when he first spoke to her of love and what they said and how they planned to marry as soon as the old laird could be persuaded to give his consent to the match. Although he was against it, they thought he might be brought over in time.

But they had no time, poor young things! Soon after, the diary told of the letter that John the

Carrier had brought her, that had frightened her terribly. And the next page said only, "My love is dead." Page after page was empty after that. Then towards the end of the little book she had written: "I know that I am going to die. I asked my father today to promise to beg the laird to let me lie beside my love when I am dead, but he only turned away and would not answer. I am afraid his pride will not let him ask a favour of one who would not accept me into his family. But, oh, my love, if he does not, I'll find a way to bring things right. I'll never rest until I do."

And that was all.

The young man raised his eyes from the page and repeated thoughtfully, "I'll never rest until I do."

It was then and there that he began to believe in ghosts!

He put the diary and the letter into his pocket, and leaving everything just as it was in the garret, he went downstairs. The packing could wait for another day. He had something better to do. As he went he thought of the old lawyer living there day after day with the ghost of his dead daughter mutely beseeching him to do what his pride would never let him do.

"Well, I have no pride at all," the young man said.

He packed a bag and put on his hat and coat, and started for the station. But as he went out of the door, he turned and put his head back in and called, "Do not fret yourself any longer, lass! You can rest now. I'll find the way to bring things right."

At the station he was fortunate enough to find a train that would take him where he wanted to go. When he got off the train he asked about the village for news of the laird. Och, the old laird was long dead, folk told him, and a rare old amadan that one was, though they shouldn't be saying it of the dead. But the new laird, him that was the old laird's nephew, had the estate now, and a finer man you'd not be finding should you search for a year and a day.

So up to the castle the young man went. When he got there he found the new laird as reasonable a man as he could hope to find. So he gave him the letter and the diary and let him read the story for himself. Then he told him about his house and the ghost in it that would not rest until she had her way.

The old laird's nephew listened gravely, and at the end of the young man's story he sighed and said, "Fifty years! Fifty long years! What a weary time to wait. Poor lass."

The old laird's nephew believed in ghosts himself.

He called his solicitors at once and got them to work. They were so quick about it that by the time the young man got back home after paying a visit to the old laird's nephew who asked him to stay till all was settled, the two lovers were reunited at last and lay together side by side in the old laird's family tomb.

When he got home he could tell the minute he stepped through the door that there was no one there but himself. There was no more trouble with the doors, and the only sounds were the ordinary sounds that he made himself.

He finally persuaded the lass he wanted to marry to come for supper one night and bring along the old aunt she lived with. The aunt prided herself on having such a keen scent for ghosts that she could actually smell one if it was in a house. So they came, and as soon as they were all settled at the supper table the aunt looked all around the rooms and sniffed two or three times.

"Ghosts! Nonsense, my dear!" she said to the young man's lass firmly. "There isn't a single ghost in this house. You may be sure I'd know at once, if there were!"

That satisfied the young lady. So, soon she and the young man were married. They lived together so happily in the house that folks completely forgot that it had ever been said that it was haunted. It didn't look at all like the kind of house that would ever have a ghost. Only the young man remembered.

He really did believe in ghosts, after all.

The King Stone

Margaret Biggs

"Oh look, Ross, there it is!" cried Meg, grabbing my arm as we leant on the steamer rail.

Suddenly the thick sea-mist was lifting, and the boat was near enough to the Isle of Arran for us to see Goat Fell starkly uprising against the windy grey sky. Immediately I felt an odd pang, a thrill of fear and bewildering recognition.

"Doesn't it look wild, Ross," Meg said, while the wind tore at our hair and the gulls hovered, screaming, overhead. She shivered and pulled her anorak tighter around her. "Look at all the mountains with the mist around them!" She paused. "Do you think we'll like it here?"

"Don't worry, it'll be all right," I said, acting bored.

We were going to stay on a farm on the island for a fortnight. Meg had been ill, and Mum couldn't get

away from her job, so I was in charge. I didn't mind –
I was fond of Meg and used to bossing her and
keeping an eye on her. I was three years older than
her, and fourteen is pretty adult, after all, as I told
Mum when she fussed a bit.

Now the steamer was cutting swiftly through the
grey-blue water, leaving a line of creamy foam to
disappear in our wake. Brodick harbour was coming
closer, and we would soon be there. The boat's
hooter wailed, people on the quayside moved
forward, and in a few minutes we were tying up and
unloading. I gazed at the clustered houses. No, I had
never seen *them* before – yet the bleak heights of
Goat Fell looming above us made me unaccountably
tense and on edge. It was strange, because Meg was
usually the one whose imagination took wing, and I
usually the one who brought her back to earth.

I glanced at our map. Beside Goat Fell lay more
curves and heads – the Sleeping Warrior, according
to the map, undoubtedly shaped like a stretched-out
recumbent figure. My eyes lingered on the hills.
Brodick village looked a peaceful, tranquil little
place – but those hills towering above were utterly
different, timeless and menacing.

We clattered down the gangway, swinging our
bags. There was a salty tang in the air, a sense of
freedom and emptiness. It was another world from

the Midlands, which we had left early that morning. Our family was Scottish, but we had never been over the border before.

"Mum said Mr McLellan would meet the boat," Meg breathlessly reminded me, at my heels.

"That's probably him, waving," I answered, seeing a brown-faced, burly man leaning against the bonnet of an ancient car.

"So here you are! Give me those bags."

A couple of minutes later we were out of the village and driving along the String, the road that cut in curves through the centre of the island. Mr McLellan bumped us along, sometimes waving a brown arm at one of the hills as he called out a Gaelic name. The hills reared up on either side of the steeply rising mountain road. We saw sheep, who lifted their heads to stare at us as we passed, but no red deer – they were higher up, and the mist was hiding them, Mr McLellan told us. There were plenty of them, and a fine nuisance to the crops they were every spring! It was all very well for visitors to rave about them, but they'd broken his fences many a time.

After a few miles we swung off the String on to a smaller, rougher lane, which bounced us gradually back down to sea level. Now we could see the sea surrounding us on three sides. To the other lay open moorland, pale green with darker green bracken and boggy patches, and long grass straining in the keen wind, and an air of utter remoteness. Invisible above us, birds were calling in high-pitched wails – curlews, Mr McLellan told us. "Yon's Machrie Moor," he added laconically.

Looking at it I felt again, more strongly, that strange stab of remembrance mixed with fear. I gazed at the moor, expecting, yet dreading, to see something. Why on earth should this lonely place summon up such feelings? I was angry with myself. It was stupid. Had I seen a picture of the moor somewhere, and forgotten it?

Down, down the lane, and on nearer the sea, and then at last a twisty turn up a stony path, and we jerked into the lonely croft where the McLellans lived, and Mrs McLellan took visitors sometimes. A friend had given Mum her address, and said it was just the spot for Meg to get strong again after scarlet fever. We got out stiffly, and the wind whipped at our hair. The moor lay close all around the small low croft. The gulls swooped and cried over our heads. It was the edge of the world.

"I love it, don't you?" Meg said in my ear, her blue eyes glowing.

I nodded – but my feelings were hopelessly mixed, and I couldn't untangle them. It was beautiful – but threatening.

Mrs McLellan came out, small and plump and smiling, wreathed in an old-fashioned apron. She said tea was all ready, with fresh eggs and cream and jam on fresh-baked scones, and would we like to take our cases upstairs? Up the few narrow stairs we went, and I ducked my head just in time to miss a wooden beam. There were two tiny rooms up there, side by side.

"Can I have this one, Ross? It looks out on the sea," Meg said eagerly, her face looking pinker and less drawn already. She always loved the sea.

"All right, I don't mind. This one's just as good." I went into the other little room, ducking my head again under the lintel. The whitewashed ceiling was bumpy and low. I dumped my case and went over to the window. The casement stood open, the faded curtains flapped. I leaned out, and a shudder shook my whole body. Beyond, on the moor, perhaps two hundred yards away, stood an incomplete circle of dark grey, weathered, standing stones.

Danger – danger! screamed a voice in my head. Hide! Angrily I stared at the stones. They drew and held my gaze irresistibly. Silent, motionless, brooding, like untiring watchers they stood waiting – waiting for what? My eyes settled uneasily on the tallest, a head taller than the others. It faced the croft squarely, leaning forward, its shape like humped shoulders. I scowled at it, fighting down a sick, queasy feeling.

I had seen the stones before. I knew too well the shape of each one, but the tallest was the one I dreaded most of all, the one I had to drag my eyes away from.

I said nothing to Meg, of course, and over tea we got chatting to the McLellans, and I tried to concentrate on what they were saying. Their children had grown up and gone away to live on the mainland, Mrs McLellan told us, but she and her husband would never leave. They had been born here, and the island was in their blood. Their eldest son wanted them to sell up and go to Glasgow with him – but no, they would stay where they were. Machrie was the place for them. The loneliness never troubled them.

We were tired after our long journey, too tired to explore that night. It was still light when we went yawning up to bed. We were so far west, Mr McLellan told us, it was light until midnight at midsummer. Even now, in the spring, it was light till almost eleven. That seemed uncanny. In my pyjamas I drew back the curtains before getting into bed. There were the stones, silhouetted and watching against the darkening sky. I stared at them for a long moment, and I was uncomfortably aware of their power. Hastily I snatched the curtains across again.

I didn't want to see them – and I didn't want them to see me.

I fell asleep quickly in Mrs McLellan's thyme-scented, darned sheets. Soon I began to dream. I dreamt of the stones. They were calling to me, lumbering heavily towards me, encircling me so that I couldn't escape. They grew larger and larger, crowding and jostling round me. Then one of them spoke, and I knew which one it was.

"Come, you must come. I am waiting for you. I have waited a long time," he said slowly.

At these words I woke up with a violent jerk. My face was sweaty, and my hands. I found I was

clutching the pillow tightly. I lay hearing my heart thump, and tried to calm down. Meg sometimes had bad dreams that frightened her, but never me. It was a long time before I fell asleep again.

Next day was bright and clear and windy. After breakfast we set out for the seashore, half a mile away. Meg was interested in seabirds, and Mrs McLellan told her we would see some rare ones if we watched. The stony beach was deserted, and we sat at the water's edge and pulled off our trainers to dabble our feet. It was surprisingly warm, and so clear we could see tiny crabs running below, and strands of green and brown weed moving like flags in the current, twining round the rocks. Flocks of wild duck bobbed on the waves. To the east a little river, Machrie Water, gurgled in a narrow channel into the quiet sea. I had never been in such a peaceful spot. I began to relax.

"I do love it here," Meg said. "It could be a Stone Age beach, Ross, couldn't it?"

A warning bell rang in my mind. Stone – the Stones . . . I shivered, although I wasn't cold, and lay back and shut my eyes. I felt tired, and that was rare for me. What *was* the matter with me – was I starting scarlet fever myself?

"You do like it, don't you?" Meg said anxiously. She set great store by my opinion.

"Yes, of course," I said, and rolled on to my stomach. I didn't want to talk. Meg chattered on, about all the things we could do, climb the hills, go on the bus to Brodick, how we must send cards to Mum and tell her how beautiful it was here. I listened. I felt far away from her, as if I was turning into somebody different. I rolled a smooth, heavy stone in my hand, and thought of hunting red deer, running after them with a handful of stones, and that was strange, for I hated all forms of hunting.

As we walked back to the croft for dinner, Meg caught sight of the stones. The sun was glinting on them, and they looked silvery, innocent. "Oh, Ross, shall we go and look?" she said.

I set my jaw. "Don't be daft, it's dinner time. They're only old stones."

"Your voice sounds funny," Meg said, peering sideways at me. "I know they're only stones, but they're fascinating. Somebody must have put them there, centuries ago. What for, do you think?"

"I don't know and I don't care," I said, taking her arm and lugging her along. "Come on, I want my dinner."

But while we ate, Meg had to question Mrs McLellan about the stones. Mrs McLellan was evasive, I thought. Nobody knew much about the stones, she said. She didn't like them herself, and never went near them. "A burying place, some say that's what they are," she said. She cut us slices of fruit pie, and paused before she added, "They're best left to themselves. Sandy, our old dog, never goes nigh them."

"One's much bigger than all the rest, isn't it?" said Meg.

Again the hesitation. "That's the King Stone," Mrs McLellan answered quietly. "Now help yourselves to some of my custard."

I reached out for the jug and saw that my fingers were trembling. The King Stone – a good name for him. Why did I think of the stone as him, not it? I felt a wave of panic. I wanted to jump up and shout, "I hate them, I hate them all, and I can't get them out of my mind!" I swallowed, feeling half choked.

Mrs McLellan was looking at me curiously. "You'll break the handle," she said, and took the jug from me.

I saw Meg look at me, her brow wrinkled, and then she looked down at her plate and didn't say another word. Sometimes she can guess what I'm thinking pretty accurately. At least she didn't mention the stones again, and that was a huge relief.

We caught the bus to Brodick that afternoon, and I was thankful to be among prosaic people and things. We did some shopping for Mrs McLellan, explored the village and the harbour, and chose some postcards. Meg spent ages spinning round a holder full of cards, choosing with infinite care. I never bother much over things like that, so I took a few at random without looking. Standing there outside the shop in the spring sunshine, with people chattering around me, and children clanking buckets and spades, I looked at the three I had chosen, and went very cold. Each one was of the stones on Machrie Moor. I knew then there was no escape. On each card the King Stone leapt up at me. I addressed them, scribbled a few phrases and posted them straight away, to get them out of my hands.

That night in bed I read for a long time, and kept my back turned to the window. I didn't want to go to sleep, but at last, well after midnight, my eyes were aching so much I had to put the book down. I reached out and switched off the light. A strange half-darkness filled the room as I drifted uneasily off to sleep.

Again the nightmare came, as I knew it would, and it was worse this time. The stones were nearer, and the King Stone was gigantic. His mossy, uneven surface sparkled, giving him a strange grimace. His stone shoulders spread wide, blocking out the light. In the dream I was backing away, but my bare feet were dragging and I could scarcely lift them. The stone was breathing, he was live, throbbing, and from him came the words: "You know you must come to me. I am waiting, I am tired of waiting. Come!"

I gasped, "No!" and with an unspeakable effort I forced myself to wake up.

To my horror a huge shape loomed over me, wavering. This was worse than the dream. I almost screamed. Then I saw it was the shadow cast by moonlight of the flapping curtain. I lay quivering, taking great gulping breaths to steady myself. I was so scared I almost rushed into Meg's room. But of course I didn't. I was always the one who looked after her, not the other way round. The last thing I wanted was to scare her as well. It's all in my mind, I told myself. It must be. The trouble was, I knew in my bones that wasn't true. Something implacably evil was after me, from long ago, and it was getting closer.

When I woke up, and the bright sunshine was flooding through the thin curtains, I resolved not to mess about any longer, but to take some action. I would have to go to the King Stone, though the mere thought made me shudder. But I had to do it, because it was the only way out of this frightening maze. I'll go, and touch the stone, and maybe that will make everything normal and sane again, I thought.

A stone can't be alive, can't have power. I'll go today, and prove it.

But when? I knew I had to go alone, and Meg wanted us to go out for the day, exploring the caves near Blackwaterfoot, the next village. Mrs McLellan had promised to pack us a big picnic lunch, and it was all arranged. Well, I would have to go that night, that was all.

We tramped along the beach to the caves, and I felt much better and more like myself, the further we got away from Machrie Moor. We met nobody else, and sang loud nonsense songs that set the gulls shrieking indignantly, and threw flat stones into the sea to make them skim. Meg beamed on me occasionally and seemed pleased.

"This is fun, isn't it, Ross? It's a perfect holiday," she said, as we sprawled eating our sandwiches in the sunshine. "P'raps we can come again some time with Mum."

"No, thanks," I said brusquely. "I'd rather go somewhere else."

"I wish you'd tell me what's worrying you," Meg said.

"What rubbish. Don't be crazy," I said.

"But, Ross, I might be able to help—" she began beseechingly.

"Shut up!" I snapped. "Shut *up*!" I rarely shouted at her, and I felt mean, but I had to. How could I tell her about the stones, and the way they were haunting me? It would only worry and scare her.

After that the day was spoilt. We reached the caves and explored them, and then wandered round the village at Blackwaterfoot, but we said little to each other. As a peace-offering, I asked Meg if she'd like an ice, but she refused, and by mid-afternoon we had turned back towards Machrie Moor. With every step, the terror came back to me.

It was a question of killing time now, waiting until I could go to the stones. We played cards with the McLellans all evening, and I tried to throw myself into it. The clock hands moved slowly onwards, and all too soon it was ten o'clock, and we all went up to bed.

There was a full moon rising, brightening in the sky as the daylight faded. I sat by the window watching the darkness come creeping across the moor. At midnight I would go. I was full of a strange exaltation now. Why had I felt so scared? I had to go – it was the right thing. The house was utterly still when at last I went slowly down the creaky stairs. Nothing could have stopped me.

I unlocked the door and closed it gently behind me, and went steadily on to the stones. They seemed nearer the house, to be beckoning me. The moonlight poured peacefully down on them, and their long, crooked shadows slanted across the moor towards me. The longest shadow came from the King Stone. I felt at peace now. Steadily I walked on into the circle, and came right up to the stone. I stood in the circle facing the King Stone.

"You see. I've come. I'm not afraid," I said, and laid both hands on the cold rough surface.

Then, in a flash, everything changed. My hands clung to the King Stone, and I couldn't tear them away. The King Stone was pulling me closer, hanging on to me. He had got me! And round the others there were people dressed in skins, some carrying blazing torches, chanting and dancing. The noise was overwhelming. They were dancing round the stones, round and round, and gradually and relentlessly they drew nearer till they were dancing round the King Stone alone. Smoke from the torches singed my eyes, the loud chanting deafened me, the faces flashing past, nearer and nearer to me, were lit up in the glare, full of excitement, snarling with anticipation. There was no pity in any of them. I struggled to pull myself away, but the power of the King Stone bound me, as if I was tied up in ropes. Then I saw a tall, dark-skinned man move very near, still chanting as he raised his spear. I saw how it shone in the moonlight, especially the jaggedly sharp pointed tip. And I knew all this had happened to me once before, long, long ago. The savage,

contorted face, the blazing eyes, the burnished spear, I remembered everything now. In a moment I would lie dead at the foot of the merciless King Stone, and he would at last be satisfied. There was nothing I could do, nobody to help me.

I felt utterly lonely. The stars above me spun jerkily as I lifted my head, trying frenziedly to pull away. The moon reeled before my eyes. Then, as the spear flashed down towards my chest, I fainted. It was no use trying any more. It was all over. The King Stone had triumphed.

"Ross! Ross!"

It was Meg's voice, from another world. Slowly, reluctantly, I drifted back to consciousness. I was lying in the grass beyond the stone circle where she must have dragged me, and she was kneeling over me, crying and shaking me.

"Oh, Ross, do wake up – *please*!"

I sat up very slowly, realizing the spear had never reached me. The night was perfectly still, so still I could hear the waves washing on the beach half a mile away, and there was only Meg and myself. Her face was chalky white in the moonlight.

"I heard you come downstairs, and I came after you. I knew there was something wrong. Oh, Ross, are you all right? Why were you twisting about against the stone like that?"

"Didn't you see them all?" I said dazedly, but I knew she hadn't.

"I had to pull and pull to get you away from the King Stone. I was scared, but I knew something awful would happen if I didn't. You looked dreadful! And suddenly the stone let you go." She was shivering. "Oh, Ross, let's get away from them!"

I stood up, and my legs felt like jelly. "Tomorrow we'll make some excuse and get away from the island – go home," I whispered shakily. "They'll always be waiting for me while I stay – especially *him*. I can't explain, Meg, but we must."

Blessedly, Meg didn't ask any questions, simply nodded in acceptance, and squeezed my icy hand.

We walked back towards the croft, keeping well away from the stones. But the power had gone, and even the King Stone, when I dared to glance at him, had lost his malevolence. Or had he? Was it a trick? Hand in hand we reached the croft door, and looked back. The stones seemed to have shrunk, to be sleeping in the moonlight. They had lost for now.

But I knew too well they would always be waiting for me. Always, till the end of my life.

Someone Drowned

Tony Richards

Danger!

The sign was huge, the warning painted in large black letters on a white background. Fixed to a solid metal post, it stuck out of the water just downstream of the weir. The river widened and deepened there, where the powerful current had cut a weirpool out of the raw earth. Great care had been taken in placing the sign. Wherever you stood, it was the first thing which caught your eye. *Danger!*

It was evening, a long, hot, summer holiday evening, alive with the sounds of midges and moorhens. Jeff Hollis sat on the grassy bank of the weirpool, his fishing rod in his hand. As the light faded, the red tip of his float became harder to see. He strained his eyes trying to watch it. But, every so often, his gaze would wander to the sign, inspecting it guiltily. His parents and his teachers had warned him about coming here. A policeman had chased him off once. The weirpool was very deep and dangerously strong, he knew that the adults were right to worry.

Someone – a young boy no older than Jeff – had drowned here last summer. The river had become a raging torrent after a heavy storm, and the boy had been sucked helplessly under.

But still Jeff and his friends Tom and Leon came to the weirpool each day through the hole under the tall wire fence. They got wet and tore their clothes, got told off when they went home. It did not bother them. They were drawn here, to this secret and magical place. It beckoned them.

In the centre of the town, an adventure playground had been built to keep the children amused during the summer holidays. Jeff and Tom and Leon never used it, never even thought of using it. A dead thing, full of planks and ropes and big discarded tyres. No privacy there. It was everyone's. The weirpool was theirs alone. They could run splashing along the slippery shelf of the weir. They could fish in the pool. They could swim, fighting the current, braving the full might of the river. This spring, they had even built a raft out of boards and empty oil drums. It lay moored beneath an overhanging willow tree. Jeff could hear the muted thump of the steel drums against the bank as the raft wafted to and fro.

His thoughts were wandering. He realized that he had time for one more cast. Tom and Leon would be here soon to join him in a night swim. He reeled in his tackle, checked the bait, then cast out again for the deepest, darkest area of the pool.

Around the float, the water eddied and swirled. The teachers had said that it was twenty feet deep, and Jeff could well believe them. It looked black as oil, impenetrable to the gaze, and gave the impression of being bottomless. The surface glittered with wavelets and foam which formed beautiful, wild patterns. Of all the river, this place was unique.

The float was gone! A bite, at long last! Jeff lifted his rod and struck the hook home.

The rod immediately bent double.

His heart thumping, Jeff reeled in a couple of yards before realizing that the weight on the other end was lifeless and inert. A clump of weed, maybe, or a waterlogged branch. Disappointment welled up in him. He would not have a catch to show the others after all. Still, he had better get his line in.

He set to work, reeling in slowly, pointing the rod tip straight out so that it would not break. The obstruction was very large and heavy. And yet, Jeff noticed, the current was not affecting it. Whatever he had on his hook was coming directly, ponderously at him. The angle of the line showed that it was almost in. Jeff gazed down into the ebony waters, trying to see what he had caught. Something white and indefinable returned his gaze.

White? In this river?

He tugged the line, and part of the object surfaced. One part only. It had not been hooked, but was holding tightly on to the nylon line.

A hand.

Jeff yelled with fright and, dropping his rod, fell back on to the grass. He lay there, propped up on his elbows, wanting to close his eyes and finding he could not. He stared. The hand still protruded above the surface. It was small – a boy's, he guessed – and white as milk. Jeff immediately thought of the boy who had drowned last year. But the body had been found and removed. So what was this?

There was one answer to that question. An unbelievable, terrifying answer.

The line suddenly went slack. The hand had released its hold, and, as Jeff watched, it opened till the fingers were spread apart, straight. The palm gleamed ghostly pale against the dusk. Jeff wanted to scream, but his throat felt tight, his mouth dry.

The hand stayed there, above the water, for a moment longer. Then it vanished. It did not sink again, just . . . *went.*

*

"Caught anything?" asked Tom.

Jeff was huddled against a tree trunk, far away from the bank. He had been there for some time. Raising his head, he saw that his friends had arrived. Tom, slender as the willow near the pool. And beefy, bullying Leon.

"No, nothing," Jeff said feebly.

"He's caught a cold, if you ask me," said Leon in that too loud voice of his. "Look at the way he's shivering."

"On a night like this?" Tom bent down to have a closer look. "You're really pale, Jeff. Are you OK?"

"He's fine," Leon cut in. "Let's go swimming."

60

He began to strip down to his trunks. Tom, as always, copied him. They undressed in silence, leaving their clothes in an untidy pile on the grass. When, at last, they were ready, they turned to Jeff.

"Well?" asked Leon. "Are you coming in, or are you just going to sit there all night?"

"I don't think it's a good idea," Jeff replied. "It's dangerous. The sign says so."

Leon looked grim. "The sign's always been there. It's never bothered you before. So why now?"

"Come on, Leon," said Tom. "If he doesn't want to go, that's his business. Leave him."

"No," said Leon. "I think he's turned chicken."

Jeff considered telling them just what he had seen in the pool that had made him afraid to go in. But he knew that they would never believe him. They would think he was making it up because he was scared.

"All right," he said. "I'm coming. I'll show you who's chicken."

As he began to undress, the other boys dived in, splashing the sign as they went. They always splashed it. That was their way of defying it. Jeff watched them, and he realized what it really was that drew them to the pool. Not the beauty, nor the solitude, nor the secrecy. They went there because they were not supposed to, because the adults told them not to and the sign warned them off. The danger of the weirpool attracted them like moths to a flame.

Jeff knew that he could cope with almost anything the river threw at him. But the hand, rising pale and ghostly from the dark pool, presented more danger than he had bargained for.

Arriving home, he left his fishing rod in the shed and sneaked in through the back door. His mother was in the kitchen, standing by the oven, waiting for him. His father stood behind her. Their expressions were identical, wavering between anger and concern.

"Jeff," said his mother, "where have you been? Your supper's ruined."

Jeff stood still and tried to look ashamed. "Sorry. I've been playing with Tom and Leon. At the adventure playground."

Both of them stared at him disbelievingly. He became painfully aware of how transparent the lie was. His hair, he realized, was still damp. It was obvious where he had been.

Mr Hollis stepped forwards. "Come here," he said. Jeff walked to him, and his father took him gently but firmly by the shoulders. "You've been to the weirpool again, haven't you?"

Jeff nodded.

"You're stupid. Really stupid. We've warned you time after time not to go there. You'll get killed."

An answer trembled on Jeff's lips. He wanted to tell them how it felt to have a secret, private world, a haven of trees and water and solitude. How it felt to swim and ride the raft in fierce currents. How it felt actually to face danger. They would not understand. There was nothing to say. Jeff remained gloomily silent.

"I'm going to have to stop your allowance this week," his father said. "And send you to bed early, without supper."

There was a programme on the television that Jeff had particularly wanted to see. He had been waiting for it all week. His lips went tight. Mr Hollis frowned.

"Cruel world, isn't it?" he said. "It would be even crueller if you'd got into trouble in that weirpool. This is for your own good."

"You know a boy drowned there last year?" his mother added. "Yes, of course you know. Doesn't that bother you?"

Jeff was about to reply when a thought occurred to him. He asked, "What was the boy's name?"

"What an odd question," said his father. "It was Alan Weeks, if you must know. Why do you ask?"

"Just curious," said Jeff.

Mr Hollis shook his head tiredly. "For a son of mine, you're a very strange boy," he said. "Now, upstairs. And say goodnight politely."

Jeff took his leave of them and went out into the hall. He reached the foot of the staircase, then turned and went back to listen at the door.

"I don't know what to do with him," Mrs Hollis was saying. "However much we warn him, he still goes back to that dreadful place. His friends are just as bad. Perhaps if I spoke to their parents . . ."

"That's worse than useless," Jeff's father replied. "The more fuss we make, the more the boys go there. They're fascinated by it. Anyway, tomorrow I'll give the council a ring. They should have blocked up that hole ages ago."

Then footsteps came towards the door and Jeff hurried before them, running to his bed.

He thought a little while about what his parents had said. They were right, he knew, but at the same time terribly wrong. Jeff lay back on his pillow, thinking of the gleaming water and what he had seen in it. He did not expect to sleep that night.

The swim, though, and the fright, had tired him more than he realized. He soon drowsed off and fell into a deep sleep. His dreams were black, and a thousand small white hands raised themselves up through the darkness.

*

The next morning, he awoke early. The sun was rising bright in a clear, cloudless sky. The day promised to be hot. Perfect. He ate his breakfast swiftly and was heading for the front door when he caught the look on his mother's face. It would be better, he decided, not to push his luck. He got his tennis racket and ball and went to play in the back garden.

"That's better," said his mother. "Don't break any windows."

By half past ten he was bored. The garden was large and nicely kept, but it held no mystery, no wildness. He longed to be with his friends. Finally, he could stand no more. He tiptoed back inside the house. From upstairs, he could hear the noise of the vacuum cleaner. It drowned out every other sound. His mother would not be able to hear a thing. Especially not the slamming of the front door.

The bank of the pool was deserted when Jeff arrived. It was odd. Tom and Leon should have been there hours ago. An unpleasant thought came to him. Perhaps they had gone swimming – and that hand in the pool had grabbed them. That was silly. Or was it? He began to panic.

He was just about to start calling their names when the boys appeared through the trees downriver. Both were red-faced and breathless, as if they had been running. Both looked miserable.

"The raft's gone," Tom explained. "It's floated down the river, and we'll never find it now. The rope must have come undone."

"It couldn't have," Leon burst in angrily. "I moored it with a special knot my brother in the navy taught me. Someone must have untied it."

"That's crazy," Tom protested. "Who would do that?"

"Well *someone* did!" yelled Leon, his face turning from red to purple.

And Jeff had a funny idea who.

"Forget it, Leon," he said. "We can build another one."

"I suppose so," Leon replied bitterly.

They had been planning to ride the raft the whole day. Now it was gone, halfway to the sea by now, and they were left to brood. It was Tom who finally broke the silence.

"I'm hot," he said. "And sticky. How about a good long swim?"

It was a way of taking their minds off the raft. All three of them agreed and quickly stripped down to their trunks. Leon and Tom dived in first, as usual. Jeff hung back a bit, hovering at the water's edge. He could not get over the hand he had seen last night. But then, perhaps he had imagined it. The darkness could have played tricks with his eyes, or he might have drowsed off and been dreaming. Yes, just his imagination, that was all. Steeling himself, he plunged in.

The water covered him, claimed him. Below the surface, everything was cool and dark. A stream of bubbles escaped his lips, quicksilver beads which sought the light. He followed them, broke the surface and swam towards his friends. Before he knew what he was doing, he had swum over the deepest spot, the place where his float had gone down the night before.

Something brushed against his foot.

He froze and immediately began to sink. Only a weed, he reassured himself uncertainly. Gazing into the water revealed nothing. It was too dark, too black. Jeff wanted nothing more than to get away from this spot. He swam, reverting to a doggy-paddle in his fright.

Again, something touched his foot. This time it stayed and, moving up, grasped hold of his ankle.

Jeff opened his mouth to shout for help, only for it to be filled with water. The hand – he *knew* it was the hand – had dragged him under. It hauled him down, down, with incredible speed and strength. Jeff wriggled like an eel, but he could not get free. His lungs ached. He was running out of air.

The descent stopped.

Jeff found himself hovering a few feet above the mud. Through the underwater gloom, weeds loomed like octopuses, fish skittered. He should not have been able to see anything down here. The water around him was somehow filled with a strange pale light.

The grip on his ankle loosened slightly, allowing him to turn round. For the first time, he saw the owner of the hand. It was a boy of roughly his age, and it had to be Alan Weeks. Or at least, his ghost. The spectre seemed at one with the water, part of it. The body, clad in T-shirt and short trousers, wavered with the current. The fair hair flowed like a weed. The boy's skin was completely white, his eyes a startling blue-green. And he glowed.

Jeff kicked at first, then became calm. The drowned boy was staring at him carefully. There was no malice in his eyes, only anger and concern, the same expression Jeff had seen on his own parents' faces. This was no more than a warning. A very grim warning.

Jeff understood.

The spectre of Alan Weeks vanished, and so did the grip on Jeff's ankle. He shot back to the surface like a cork, came out coughing and spluttering. As soon as his breath was back he struck out for the bank.

"Hey!" his friends shouted. "Where are you going?"

They caught up with him on the bank, as he was getting dressed. Jeff told them what he had seen, what he knew. Leon did not believe him.

"You liar," he said. "You're just making this up because you're scared of the pool. Chicken, just like I said."

"I'm not," Jeff protested. "I really did see the ghost of Alan Weeks. He was warning us away."

"Why now? Why wait the whole year? We've been all right all summer, danger sign or not."

"I – I don't know," Jeff mumbled. "Perhaps he knows something that we don't. Perhaps he can see that something bad is going to happen to us."

Leon snorted and began to turn away. It was Tom who caught him by the arm and stopped him.

"Leon," he said, "maybe it's true."

Leon shrugged his hand off with contempt. "Don't you start now," he snapped. "There's no such thing as ghosts, right? He's just a coward, and if you start believing him then you're no friend of mine, ever again. Now, are you coming back in the water or not?"

The look of worry on Tom's face was intense. He was obviously not sure who to believe. But in the end he would do what Leon said. He always did.

Jeff walked home alone.

That night, the sultry weather broke. Huge, rolling clouds filled the sky towards evening, and later on a thunderstorm shook the town to its foundations. The pouring rain went on until the early morning, flooding everything.

The next day, when Jeff awoke, he was filled with an uneasy feeling. He crossed to his bedroom window and gazed out. The bright sun was slowly drying out the ground, but huge puddles still lingered here and there. The rain had been torrential. And the river, Jeff knew, would be in full flood.

Just as it had been a year ago when Alan Weeks had drowned.

That was it! Now he knew what the ghost had been trying to warn him. Only a fool would go near the weirpool today, only a madman. *Leon!* He was just brash, just stupid enough to try swimming in these conditions. Glancing at the alarm clock by his bed, Jeff saw that his friends would be at the pool by now.

He got dressed quickly and rushed for the door.

Jeff could hear the weirpool even before he saw it. The roar of water tumbling over the edge was deafening. As he drew closer, he could faintly hear another noise. A voice, Tom's voice, shouting for help. Jeff burst through the trees to see Tom standing on the bank, teetering to and fro. He was in a state of extreme panic. Fearing the worst, Jeff ran to his side and stared out across the water.

He could not see Leon at first. The weirpool was the worst he had ever seen it. The water had turned brown and was alive with foam and flotsam. It thundered, rushing past the bank, carrying everything in its wake. The trunk of a dead tree sailed by, and then Jeff caught a glimpse of a tiny black object further out. He only just recognized it as the top of Leon's head.

Jeff turned to Tom.

"Get help!" he shouted. "Move!"

As Tom broke out of his stupor and ran back for the fence, Jeff kicked off both his shoes and, without even thinking, dived in. He battered his way to the surface, took in a deep gulp of air, then fought outwards against the mighty current. The air trapped in his clothing helped at first by buoying him up, but as it seeped out the material became waterlogged. Feeling as heavy as lead, Jeff battled on. Every other stroke, the water would break over his head, threatening to carry him under. But he made it.

Wild with terror, Leon was in no state to help in his own rescue. Jeff tried to swim around behind him to get hold of his shoulders when suddenly Leon grabbed hold of him.

"No, wait!" Jeff yelled. "Let go!"

Leon was too frightened to hear. He clasped hold of Jeff, pinning his arms to his sides. They both sank like stones.

Below the surface, Jeff could still hear the noise of the water. It was louder now, filling his head, drowning him in fury. The harder he tried to free himself, the tighter Leon's grasp became. They were sinking further. Jeff knew that they would never come up again.

From behind, a strong pair of hands suddenly took

hold of his shoulders. It wasn't Leon, and Tom had gone to fetch help.

The murky water was filled with a peculiar glow.

Jeff felt himself and Leon being drawn towards the surface. Then he passed out.

He came to not long afterwards. Opening his eyes, he saw that he was lying on the bank. Tom was standing over him, and, with Tom, a policeman. Other people were rushing towards them with blankets. Beside him, Leon was coughing out water.

"You saved his life," the policeman said. "Brave lad. You'll get some kind of reward for this, I'm sure."

"No," said Jeff weakly. "Not me."

The last time Jeff visited the weirpool was after the award ceremony. He was still wearing his suit. It had got dirtied from the crawl under the fence, but nobody would mind now.

Walking through the trees, he went right up to the edge of the bank. The pool was still the same. The midges, the ripples, the never-ending blackness of the water. It would never change.

Jeff gazed at his own reflection. It was he who had changed. He had become a little more grown-up, and in exchange had given up his secret, private world. For the rest of his life, he would never return. He felt he owed that to the pool's inhabitant.

And there was something else he owed.

He fished in his trouser pocket and drew out a black, leather-bound box. A gleam of gold escaped as he opened it. Cushioned on red satin inside was the medal the mayor had presented to him an hour ago. He took it out and turned it over in his hand, reading the inscription. It bore his name. That was a mistake, and only he could put it right.

"It belongs to you, not me," Jeff whispered across the pool. "Thank you."

He threw the medal out towards the deepest area of the pool. It splashed, glimmered once, and then was gone. Into darkness.

Can't Help Laughing

Alison Prince

Outside the Maths Hut, a bird was tugging a worm out of the earth, leaning backwards with the worm stretched like tight elastic. Sophie watched through the window. It'll go ping in a minute, she thought, and the bird will fall on its bum. She giggled.

"Sophie Mayhew, get on with your work," snapped Miss Webb. Sophie looked at her and thought what a peevish little mouth the teacher had, its corners running down into the sagging lines of her cheeks. It was the first time they had been taught by Miss Webb. Last term Mr Thompson had taken them for Maths. He was young and cheerful – not a bit like Miss Webb, who looked like a bad-tempered Pekinese. A grin crept across Sophie's face at this thought, and she glanced out of the window again to try and hide it. Outside, the worm came out of the earth with an almost audible plop and the bird fell over backwards. Sophie burst into fits of giggles.

"Sophie!" Miss Webb's jowls shook with anger. "What, may I ask, is so funny?"

"Nothing," said Sophie, trying to pull her face straight.

"I can hardly see that you have anything to smirk about," spat Miss Webb. "Your attainment in this subject would do no credit to a backward five-year-old. You will report to me after school. Perhaps when you are working on your own you will find it a little less – *funny*." She pronounced the last word with extreme dislike.

"Yes, miss," said Sophie. It was not the first time she had been in trouble for giggling, but she could never help laughing when something struck her as funny. Her friends made sympathetic faces, and one of the boys muttered, "Who's a naughty girl, then?" Miss Webb glared at him but said nothing. Everyone knew that she was never quite so nasty to the boys, probably because she had taught in the Girls' Grammar School all her life – that is, until it became part of the Comprehensive. Rather like a cavalry officer having to drive a tank, Sophie thought. She very nearly giggled again.

Being in detention was particularly dreadful on a summer afternoon. The Maths Hut smelt frowsty and, now that everyone had gone home, the school was silent except for the cheerful whirr of the mower as Mr Atkins, the caretaker, rode round and round the field and the wide cutters tossed up a cloud of grassy dust behind the machine.

"I am going to the staffroom for a few minutes," Miss Webb announced tightly. "I shall want to see your work when I return."

Sophie watched her go out. She hated Miss Webb. She hated the solid, tweed-encased body, the plump fingers, the high carriage of the sagging chin which somehow implied that life was full of nasty smells. When the door closed behind the teacher, Sophie put her pen down and leaned back in her chair, stretching her arms above her head. The very air of the Maths Hut seemed to relax in Miss Webb's absence. Sophie opened the window and leaned out. The sweet, delicious scent of the mown grass poured in. "M'm," said Sophie. "Lovely." I wonder what the old bat's gone down to the staffroom for, she added to herself.

"Needs a wee, I expect." The comment came in a confidential whisper, just behind Sophie's shoulder, and was followed by a raucous cackle.

Sophie jumped round and stared into the empty room. She looked suspiciously up at the fanlight above the door. There was nobody to be seen.

"Only human, aren't they?" said the voice. It was as intimate as though the owner stood at Sophie's elbow, nudging her. The hair rose on the back of Sophie's neck. Trying to ignore the fact that the voice was so close, she told herself that she must be overhearing a conversation outside. She got up and went to the door.

"No use looking out there," said the voice, still close beside her. "I'm here, silly."

Sophie felt embarrassed as well as scared. This sort of thing did not happen. There must be a reasonable explanation. She looked around the room again, thinking suspiciously of tape recorders or radios.

"Oh, do sit down, dear," said the voice. "It makes my feet tired, you walking about like this. I used to have terrible trouble with my feet. 'Course, I'm lighter now, you might say. Ha-ha-ha-ha-ha!" Sophie nearly laughed as well, although she was breathless with alarm. And what was so funny about being lighter now?

"I knew you was my sort this morning, when you got the giggles," the voice went on. "That's why I've chosen you to talk to. Madam got proper upset, didn't she?"

Sophie glanced round, still very alarmed and half-convinced that the whole thing was some kind of trick. To say something would be to admit that she could hear the voice – but she could think of no other way to find out what was going on. "Who are you?" she whispered aloud.

"They call me Lil," said the voice cheerfully. "No, you can't help laughing, can you, the fuss some of these teachers make."

Sophie gave a scared, breathless laugh, then blushed, still afraid that she was the victim of some practical joke.

"Now, look, dear," said Lil in a matter-of-fact tone, as close to Sophie's ear as though she had her arm around the girl's shoulders, "there's no need to panic. People are so silly about ghosts. We don't all go moaning around in a grey mist, you know. Ha-ha-ha!"

"You're a – ghost?" said Sophie, her voice rising to a squeak.

"Well, what do you *think* I am?" said Lil impatiently. "And don't pretend you're scared – you're not the scary sort, otherwise you wouldn't be here. You're only in detention because you weren't frightened of the old battle-axe – so why be frightened of me? I wouldn't hurt a fly."

"Wouldn't you?" Though half reassured, Sophie still sounded rather shaky.

" 'Course not," said Lil. "Ha! I don't say I wouldn't

like to, but I just don't have the weight for it. Ha-ha! A ghost is no blooming good as a fly swat!"

Sophie could not help joining in with Lil's roar of laughter. The door was flung open and Miss Webb stood there. Sophie at once tried to put on a suitably grave expression, but Miss Webb swelled like an angry bluebottle.

"Here we go," muttered Lil as the teacher advanced. "Fuss."

Sophie put her hand to her mouth, trying to smother a further giggle. She had suddenly seen what Lil meant about being lighter now. You couldn't have anything much lighter than a ghost. Her diaphragm shook with amusement.

Miss Webb gave no sign of having heard Lil. "You are either extremely stupid or just plain insolent," she said to Sophie. "Shut that window at once. I did not give you permission to open it."

Sophie got up, trying to control her face. The sensation of having an unseen person in the room made her feel quite hysterical.

"Got on her high horse now," observed Lil cheerfully.

"Shut up!" muttered Sophie.

Miss Webb heard her. "I *beg* your pardon!" she shouted, outraged.

"I didn't mean you, miss," said Sophie. "I'm sorry,

I sort of—"

"Put me foot in it," finished Lil. "Ha-ha-ha!"

Sophie collapsed into giggles.

"You appear to have taken leave of your senses," said Miss Webb icily. "You are perhaps an object of pity rather than contempt, but don't imagine you can get away with such behaviour. I shall expect an apology from you tomorrow, when you have recovered some semblance of mental stability."

"Nasty," said Lil.

"Meanwhile," Miss Webb continued, oblivious, "I shall waste no further time with you. You may go."

"Yes, miss," said Sophie. Still shaking with horrified amusement, she pushed her books into her bag and fled. "Goodnight," she said over her shoulder.

"Bye-bye, love," said Lil comfortably.

Miss Webb said nothing.

Sophie told Sharon, her closest friend, about Lil the next morning. Sharon looked at her with wide eyes and said, "You mean the Maths Hut is *haunted*?"

"No," said Sophie. "Not exactly. But – well, yes, I suppose it is."

"Get off," said Sharon contemptuously. "You don't get ghosts in modern buildings like this, only in old castles and things. You just imagined it."

Sophie looked at her friend and decided not to

pursue the point. If Sharon didn't believe it, nobody would. "I suppose I must have done," she said. "You won't tell anyone, will you? I'll get sent up rotten if the boys find out."

"'Course I won't," said Sharon. "I don't want people saying my friend is a nutcase, do I?"

"No," agreed Sophie meekly. Sharon's words echoed disturbingly in her mind. *Was* she a nutcase? She pushed the thought away firmly. A nutcase would never have invented a ghost that *laughed*.

Maths was the last lesson of the afternoon. When Miss Webb came in she beckoned to Sophie with a plump, imperious finger and, when the girl stood in front of her, said, "Well?"

Thus prompted, Sophie said, "I'm sorry about yesterday."

"I should think so," said Miss Webb. "If there is any repetition of such behaviour, you will go straight to the headmaster, do you understand?"

Among ironic groans and sighs from the boys, Sophie said obediently, "Yes, miss."

"Three bags full, miss," chipped in Lil loudly. "Ha-ha-ha!" There was a shout of amusement from the boys and everyone craned their necks to see where the voice came from.

Sophie gave a gasp of horror. There had been no sound from Lil that day, and she had begun to feel sure that whatever had happened during her detention last night had been an isolated incident, never to be repeated. But now – what?

Miss Webb glared at her suspiciously, and Sophie quickly turned the gasp into a cough. "Sorry," she said, scuttling back to her place. Sharon was scribbling on a scrap of paper which she pushed over to Sophie's desk. On it she had written, "THREE BAGS FULL???!"

So Sharon could hear Lil's voice. Everyone could hear it. Sophie's skin prickled as she looked at her friend and nodded. Who was the nutcase now? The boys were still laughing and the girls were staring round the room and giggling. Miss Webb, ignoring the noise, was writing an equation on the board, her back to the class. Still looking at Sharon, Sophie touched her own ears, pointed at the teacher and shook her head. Sharon shrugged hugely, spreading her hands. No, Miss Webb couldn't hear the voice.

"Tell you the truth," said Lil, loudly but confidentially, "I never took to Big Fat Spider Webb. Ha-ha!"

Amid the shrieks of amusement, Sophie reflected with some relief that Lil no longer sounded as if she was standing at Sophie's side, whispering into her ear. She was speaking to the whole class. Miss Webb's hand paused when the laughter broke out.

She checked her figures quickly to see that she had not made a mistake which might have caused the amusement, then swung round to face the class. Among all the excited faces, Sophie Mayhew's was the only one which was struggling to look innocent. "Stand up!" she snapped at the girl. Sophie, pinkfaced, did as she was told.

"You will go to prison for twenty years," said Lil gloomily. "Ha-ha-ha!" The class exploded into a gale of laughter, and even Sophie could not repress a panic-stricken giggle. Miss Webb's cheeks turned a dull crimson. "No doubt you think you are very clever," she snarled at Sophie. "I have no idea how you are managing to induce this disorder in the class, but I doubt if Mr Craig will share your inflated opinion of yourself. Go to his office at once. And the rest of you, get on with your work."

"Now you done it," said Lil. Her laughter and that of the class faded as Sophie closed the door of the hut behind her, but renewed shouts of amusement were clearly audible as she set off for the head teacher's office.

Sophie knocked on the door and heard the bell on Mr Craig's desk ping as a signal to enter. With a lurch of the heart, she went in. Mr Craig's bushy hair was white, his glasses as thick as bottle-bottoms. He sat behind his large desk and said nothing.

"Er – Miss Webb sent me," said Sophie.

"Yes?" Mr Craig said unhelpfully.

"I – well – everyone was laughing."

"At what?"

Sophie blushed. "I know it sounds silly," she said, "but there was a voice. Saying funny things."

Mr Craig's glasses glinted as he tilted his head at a sarcastic angle. "Like Joan of Arc?" he enquired.

"No," said Sophie. Joan of Arc could never have heard anything like Lil.

Mr Craig's glasses looked at Sophie for a moment. She wondered what his eyes were like behind them. Then he said, "Do you really expect me to believe this story?"

"No," said Sophie honestly. "But it's true."

There was a pause. "Can the others hear this – voice?" asked Mr Craig.

"Yes," said Sophie. "That's why they're laughing. But Miss Webb can't."

The headmaster sat back in his chair, tapping a pencil inconsequentially on his desk. "I think this voice is something to do with you," he said.

Sophie watched the pencil tapping, and shook her head. "I don't want it to be," she told him.

"So I shall hold you responsible for it," continued Mr Craig, ignoring her. He put the pencil into a glass tray with several others, snapping it down with a sharp click. Sophie transferred her gaze unwillingly to his glasses.

"Go back to your lesson," said Mr Craig, "and let me hear no more of this nonsense."

"But—" began Sophie.

Mr Craig leaned forward. "Don't push your luck," he said with menace.

"No, sir," said Sophie, and crept out.

Mr Atkins, the caretaker, was walking down the corridor studying the list of jobs on his clipboard. "Hello," he said at the sight of Sophie's downcast face. "Been in trouble?"

"It's not my fault," protested Sophie. "Someone keeps laughing in the Maths Hut." She knew Mr

Atkins quite well because he and Sophie's father flew racing pigeons together.

"One of your class, d'you mean?" asked Mr Atkins.

"No." Sophie frowned. Although the others thought it was so funny, there was something about Lil which she found upsetting. "It's a voice. Someone called Lil. The others can hear it but Miss Webb can't, and everyone thinks it's my fault."

"Lil?" Mr Atkins was staring at her. "Are you sure?"

"That's what she said." Sophie gulped. "She sounds ever so funny and sort of nice, but I wish in a way it hadn't happened. I feel as if I'm – well – nuts."

"The Maths Hut," repeated Mr Atkins. "Well, I'm blowed. Lily Barnum." He rubbed his forehead in perplexity.

"What do you mean?" asked Sophie.

The caretaker looked at her consideringly, as if trying to decide whether to tell her something.

"Oh, go on," Sophie begged. "Please!"

"Lily Barnum was one of our cleaners," said Mr Atkins, making up his mind. "The others called her Laughing Lil. Funny woman. She couldn't read or write – lived in a caravan on the edge of the Common. I think she hated schools, really, but she needed the money from the cleaning job. She used to laugh at the teachers, and some of them got really cross with her. You couldn't be cross with Lil for long, though. Not the way she laughed."

Sophie nodded. She knew. "What happened to her?" she asked.

"Well—" Mr Atkins hesitated again. "You won't be upset, will you? The fact is, she was found dead in the Maths Hut. Face down, with a mop in her hand. It turned out she'd had a heart condition for years, and the other cleaners said she'd had some sort of disagreement with Miss Webb. Maybe they got really angry with each other and it was too much for her heart. I never really got to the bottom of it – but we all missed old Lil." He stared at Sophie curiously. "And you say you heard her talking to you?"

"I don't know." Somehow Sophie wanted time to think about what Mr Atkins had said. She regretted confiding in him so impulsively. Although Mr Atkins was very nice, his concern made Sophie feel self-conscious. Mr Craig had simply not believed her, but Mr Atkins did, and Sophie realized afresh that what she had told him was very, very odd. "I certainly heard something," she said lightly. "Perhaps it was the record player next door." She gave what she hoped was a cheery smile.

"The Maths Hut doesn't have a next door," said Mr Atkins. Sophie wished he would stop looking at her in that worried sort of way.

"Oh. No, of course it doesn't." She smiled again, rather wildly. "How silly. Gosh, I must go or I'll get into more trouble." She fled, leaving Mr Atkins where he stood, frowning after her.

She dived through the swing doors into the safe haven of the toilets and leaned her hands on the cold edge of one of the wash basins, staring unseeingly at her reflection in the mirror. Lil could not read or write. No wonder the sight of people studying books all day seemed so funny to her. She must have said something cheeky to Miss Webb. Sophie could imagine the response all too clearly. "Oh, yes, Mrs Barnum? I suppose your fluent command of written English gives you the right to be insolent, does it?" The sarcastic voice rang in her ears.

She made her way back to the Maths Hut as slowly as she dared. She was beginning to dread meeting Lil again. There was something nightmarish about the constant laughter. As she approached the hut she could hear screams of amusement. Girls were shrieking and boys were shouting and banging the desk tops. It sounded as if the whole class was in complete hysterics. Sophie ran up the wooden steps and pushed open the door.

"Well, I told her," Lil was saying conversationally, "it's no use you coming the lah-di-dah with *me*. You may be very natty with your blooming books, I says, but who needs them? Not me, for a start-off. Ha-ha-ha! Poor old bird. She looked that took aback, I had to smile." The class collapsed in fresh fits of laughter. Miss Webb, who was clearly unable to hear a word that Lil was saying, stood leaning her knuckles on the edge of her desk, fighting for control of the class. "Be quiet at once!" she shouted. "I have had quite enough of this nonsense!"

Nobody took the slightest notice. Suddenly Sophie felt sorry for Miss Webb. It had gone too far. The laughter was horrible. "Lil," she said aloud, "do stop it."

There was too much noise in the room for anyone to notice what Sophie had said, but she was standing right beside Miss Webb, who heard her. She glared at Sophie and said in a voice choking with fury, "When I want you to take over the control of this class, Miss Mayhew, I will ask you. Sit down at once."

"Ha! Charming!" said Lil in the slight lull caused by Miss Webb's words.

There was a renewed explosion from the class, who were by now in such a hysterical state that the slightest thing precipitated a fresh outburst. Miss Webb stood back from her desk and Sophie saw that her hands were trembling. She sat down in her chair. Her mouth twitched, and for a moment Sophie thought that at last Miss Webb was going to join in the infectious laughter. The teacher put her hands over her face. Her shoulders heaved. Gradually, the class became quiet. Miss Webb, unable to laugh, was weeping.

"Oh, Lor'," said Lil in the sudden quiet. "That's done it. Gone too far." To Sophie's horror, the voice was close to her ear again, a husky whisper which only she could hear. "I better stick to you in future, dear. Shouldn't have bothered with those others. But we're the same sort, aren't we, you and me? We understand each other. If you get a chance, you can tell the old bag I'm sorry. Still – can't help laughing, can you? Ha-ha-ha!" Sophie shuddered.

Miss Webb got up, a handkerchief pressed to her face, and bolted out of the door. Standing up to stare furtively out, they saw her stumbling blindly along the concrete path which led to the staffroom.

"We'll have old Craig over in a minute," said one of the boys.

"Wasn't our fault, was it?" said another, sounding injured.

Books were retrieved from the floor and hurled back to their owners, and a rather breathless silence descended.

When the headmaster came into the Maths Hut to find out the cause of Miss Webb's extraordinary breakdown, the class was working industriously, every face innocent and busy. Sophie Mayhew, however, sat bolt upright in her seat by the window, with her hands pressed over her ears and her elbows sticking out sideways. Her eyes were staring.

"Sophie, what is the matter?" asked Mr Craig. For a moment the girl did not appear to have heard him. Then her face contorted in a horrified laugh. "Shut up!" she shouted. "Shut up, shut up, shut up!"

Mr Craig opened his mouth to protest, then closed it again. A sweat broke out on his face, which caused his glasses to mist over. Sophie Mayhew, he realized, was talking to somebody else. The bell rang for the end of afternoon school.

"You may go," said Mr Craig unnecessarily, for books were already being stuffed into bags. He cast an uneasy glance at Sophie, who was surrounded by urgently chattering friends, and went back to his office to ring the Educational Psychologist.

Sophie could not wait to get out of the Maths Hut and away from the voice in her ear, which had become as maddening as a buzzing insect. She did not even want to talk to Sharon. Lil's intimacy was horrifying, like a parasite lodged in her mind.

Sophie's house was within walking distance of the school, and so she set out along the road, glad that she did not have to wait with a Bus Group.

It was a tremendous relief to be alone and in silence. Sophie turned off the road to follow the footpath which led across the Common to her house. There was no sound except the wind in the silver birch trees and the faint swish of Sophie's feet as she walked across the dry grass. She wondered idly where Lil's caravan had been – not that it mattered. It was long gone by now, anyway. Tomorrow, she told herself, she would ask Mr Craig if she could be transferred to a lower maths group. She was quite bad enough at maths for the request to seem natural. That way, she never need go into the Maths Hut again, for the lower group worked in a room in the main building. She could avoid any further contact with the awful Laughing Lil, who had died in the Maths Hut. That is where she was found, face down with her mop in her hand, and that is where her spirit had to stay. So there, you old baggage, thought Sophie happily. That's fixed you.

"Don't kid yourself, love," said Lil. "We're going to be good mates, you and me. I don't mind you telling me to shut up occasionally, like you did this afternoon – I ain't easy offended. Ha-ha-ha! Can't help laughing, can you? Ha-ha-ha-ha-ha!"

Standing alone on the Common with her hands over her ears, Sophie screamed and screamed.

The Giant's Necklace

Michael Morpurgo

The necklace stretched from one end of the kitchen table to the other, around the sugar bowl at the far end and back again, stopping only a few inches short of the toaster. The discovery on the beach of a length of abandoned fishing line draped with seaweed had first suggested the idea to Cherry; and every day of the holiday since then had been spent in one single-minded pursuit, the creation of a necklace of glistening pink cowrie shells. She had sworn to herself and to everyone else that the necklace would not be complete until it reached the toaster; and when Cherry vowed she would do something, she invariably did it.

Cherry was the youngest in a family of older brothers, four of them, who had teased her relentlessly since the day she was born, eleven years before. She referred to them as 'the four mistakes', for it was a family joke that each son had been an attempt to produce a daughter. To their huge delight Cherry reacted passionately to any slight or insult whether intended or not. Their particular targets were her size, which was diminutive compared with theirs, her dark flashing eyes that could wither with one scornful look, but above all her ever-increasing femininity. Although the teasing was interminable it was rarely hurtful, nor was it intended to be, for her brothers adored her; and she knew it.

Cherry was poring over her necklace, still in her dressing gown. Breakfast had just been cleared away and she was alone with her mother. She fingered the shells lightly, turning them gently until the entire necklace lay flat with the rounded pink of the shells all uppermost. Then she bent down and breathed on each of them in turn, polishing them carefully with a napkin.

"There's still the sea in them," she said to no one in particular. "You can still smell it, and I washed them and washed them, you know."

"You've only got today, Cherry," said her mother coming over to the table and putting an arm around her. "Just today, that's all. We're off back home tomorrow morning first thing. Why don't you call it a day, dear? You've been at it every day – you *must* be tired of it by now. There's no need to go on, you know. We all think it's a fine necklace and quite long enough. It's long enough surely?"

Cherry shook her head slowly. "Nope," she said. "Only that little bit left to do and then it's finished."

"But they'll take hours to collect, dear," her mother said weakly, recognizing and at the same time respecting her daughter's persistence.

"Only a few hours," said Cherry, bending over, her brows furrowing critically as she inspected a flaw in one of her shells, "that's all it'll take. D'you know, there are five thousand, three hundred and twenty-five shells in my necklace already? I counted them, so I know."

"Isn't that enough, dear?" her mother said desperately.

"Nope," said Cherry. "I said I'd reach the toaster, and I'm going to reach the toaster."

Her mother turned away to continue the drying up.

"Well, I can't spend all day on the beach today, Cherry," she said. "If you haven't finished by the time we come away I'll have to leave you there. We've got to pack up and tidy the house – there'll be no time in the morning."

"I'll be all right," said Cherry, cocking her head on one side to view the necklace from a different angle. "There's never been a necklace like this before, not in all the world. I'm sure there hasn't." And then,

"You can leave me there, Mum, and I'll walk back. It's only a mile or so along the cliff path and half a mile back across the fields. I've done it before on my own. It's not far."

There was a thundering on the stairs and a sudden rude invasion of the kitchen. Cherry was surrounded by her four brothers who leant over the table in mock appreciation of her necklace.

"Ooh, pretty."

"Do they come in other colours? I mean, pink's not my colour."

"Bit big though, isn't it?" said one of them – she didn't know which and it didn't matter. He went on: "I mean it's a bit big for a necklace?" War had been declared again, and Cherry responded predictably.

"That depends," she said calmly, shrugging her shoulders because she knew that would irritate them.

"On what does it depend?" said her oldest brother, pompously.

"On who's going to wear it of course, ninny," she said swiftly.

"Well, who is going to wear it?" he replied.

"It's for a giant," she said, her voice full of serious innocence. "It's a giant's necklace, and it's still not big enough."

It was the perfect answer, an answer she knew

would send her brothers into fits of hysterical hilarity. She loved to make them laugh at her and could do it at the drop of a hat. Of course she no more believed in giants than they did, but if it tickled them pink to believe she did, then why not pretend?

She turned on them, fists flailing, and chased them back up the stairs, her eyes burning with simulated fury. "Just 'cos you don't believe in anything 'cept motorbikes and football and all that rubbish, just 'cos you're great big, fat, ignorant pigs . . ." She hurled insults up the stairs after them and the worse they became the more they loved it.

Boat Cove just below Zennor Head was the beach they had found and occupied. Every year for as long as Cherry could remember they had rented the same granite cottage, set back in the fields below the Eagle's Nest, and every year they came to the same beach because no one else did. In two weeks not another soul had ventured down the winding track through the bracken from the coastal path. It was a long climb down and a very much longer one up. The beach itself was almost hidden from the path that ran along the cliff top a hundred feet above. It was private and perfect and theirs. The boys swam in amongst the rocks, diving and snorkelling for hours on end. Her mother and father would sit side by side on stripy deck chairs. She would read endlessly and he would close his eyes against the sun and dream for hours on end.

Cherry moved away from them and clambered over the rocks to a narrow strip of sand in the cove beyond the rock, and here it was that she mined for the cowrie shells. In the gritty sand under the cliff face she had found a particularly rich deposit so that they were not hard to find; but she was looking for pink cowrie shells of a uniform length, colour and shape – and that was what took the time. Occasionally the boys would swim around the rocks and in to her little beach, emerging from the sea all goggled and flippered to mock her. But as she paid them little attention they soon tired and went away again. She knew time was running short. This was her very last chance to find enough shells to complete the giant's necklace, and it had to be done.

The sea was calmer that day than she had ever seen it. The heat beat down from a windless, cloudless sky; even the gulls and kittiwakes seemed to be silenced by the sun. Cherry searched on, stopping only for a picnic lunch of pasties and tomatoes with the family before returning at once to her shells.

In the end the heat proved too much for her mother and father who left the beach earlier than usual in mid-afternoon to begin to tidy up the cottage. The boys soon followed because they had tired of finding miniature crabs and seaweed instead of the sunken wrecks and treasure they had been seeking, so that by teatime Cherry was left on her own on the beach with strict instructions to keep her hat on, not to bathe alone and to be back well before dark. She had calculated she needed one hundred and fifty more cowrie shells and so far she had found only eighty. She would be back, she insisted, when she had finished collecting enough shells and not before.

Had she not been so immersed in her search, sifting the shells through her fingers, she would have noticed the dark grey bank of cloud rolling in from the Atlantic. She would have noticed the white horses gathering out at sea and the tide moving remorselessly in to cover the rocks between her and Boat Cove. When the clouds cut off the warmth from the sun as evening came on and the sea turned grey, she shivered with cold and slipped on her jersey and jeans. She did look up then and saw that the sea was angry, but she saw no threat in that and did not look back over her shoulder towards Boat Cove. She was aware that time was running short so she went down on her knees again and dug feverishly in the sand. There were still thirty shells to collect and she was not going home without them.

It was the baleful sound of a fog-horn somewhere out at sea beyond Gunnards Head that at last forced

Cherry to consider her own predicament. Only then did she take some account of the incoming tide. She looked for the rocks she would have to clamber over to reach Boat Cove again and the winding track that would take her up to the cliff path and safety, but they were gone. Where they should have been, the sea was already driving in against the cliff face. She was cut off. For many moments Cherry stared in disbelief and wondered if her memory was deceiving her, until the sea, sucked back into the Atlantic for a brief moment, revealed the rocks that marked her route back to Boat Cove. Then she realized at last that the sea had undergone a grim metamorphosis. In a confusion of wonder and fear she looked out to sea at the heaving ocean that moved in towards her, seeing it now as a writhing grey monster breathing its fury on the rocks with every pounding wave.

Still Cherry did not forget her shells, but wrapping them inside her towel she tucked them into her jersey and waded out through the surf towards the rocks. If she timed it right, she reasoned, she could scramble back over them and into the Cove as the surf retreated. And she reached the first of the rocks without too much difficulty; the sea here seemed to be protected from the force of the ocean by the rocks further out. Holding fast to the first rock she came to, and with the sea up around her waist, she waited for the next incoming wave to break and retreat. The wave was unexpectedly impotent and fell limply on the rocks around her. She knew her moment had come and took it. She was not to know that piling up far out at sea was the first of the giant storm waves that had gathered several hundred miles out in the Atlantic, bringing with it all the momentum and violence of the deep ocean.

The rocks were slippery underfoot and more than once Cherry slipped down into seething white rock pools where she had played so often when the tide was out. But she struggled on until finally she had climbed high enough to be able to see the thin strip of sand that was all that was left of Boat Cove. It was only a few yards away, so close. Until now she had been crying involuntarily, but now as she recognized the little path up through the bracken her heart was lifted with hope and anticipation. She knew that the worst was over, that if the sea would only hold back she would reach the sanctuary of the Cove. She turned and looked behind her to see how far away the next wave was, just to reassure herself that she had enough time. But the great surge of green water was on her before she could register either disappointment or fear. She was hurled back against the rock below her and covered at once by the sea. She was conscious as she went down that she was drowning, but she still clutched her shells against her chest and was glad she had enough of them at last to finish the giant's necklace. Those were her last thinking thoughts before the sea took her away.

Cherry lay on her side where the tide had lifted her and coughed until her lungs were clear. She woke as the sea came in once again and frothed around her legs. She rolled over on her back, feeling the salt spray on her face, and saw that it was night. The sky above her was dashed with stars and the moon rode through the clouds. She scrambled to her feet, one hand still holding her precious shells close to her. Instinctively she backed away from the sea and looked around her. With growing dismay she saw that she had been thrown back on the wrong side of the rocks, that she was not in Boat Cove. The tide had left only a few feet of sand and rock between her and the cliff face. There was no way back through the sea to safety. She turned round to face the cliff that she realized would be her last hope, for she remembered that this little beach vanished completely at high tide. If she stayed where she was she would surely be swept away again and this time she might not be so fortunate. But the cold seemed to have calmed her and she reasoned more deliberately now, wondering why she had not tried climbing the cliff before. She had hurried into her first attempt at escape and it had very nearly cost her her life. She would wait this time until the sea forced her up the cliff. Perhaps the tide would not come in that far. Perhaps they would be looking for her by now. It was dark. Surely they would be searching. Surely they must find her soon. After all, they knew where she was. Yes, she thought, best just to wait and hope.

She settled down on a ledge of rock that was the first step up on to the cliff face, drew her knees up to her chin to keep out the chill and waited. She watched as the sea crept ever closer, each wave lashing her with spray and eating away gradually at the beach. She closed her eyes and prayed, hoping against hope that when she opened them the sea would be retreating. But her prayers went unanswered and the sea came in to cover the beach. Once or twice she thought she heard voices above her on the cliff path, but when she called out no one came. She continued to shout for help every few minutes, forgetting it was futile against the continuous roar and hiss of the waves. A pair of raucous white gulls flew down from the cliffs to investigate her and she called to them for help, but they did not seem to understand and wheeled away into the night.

She stayed sitting on her rock until the waves

threatened to dislodge her and then reluctantly she began her climb. She would go as far as she needed to and no further. She had scanned the first few feet above for footholds and it did look quite a simple climb to begin with, and so it proved. But her hands were numbed with cold and her legs began to tremble with the strain almost at once. She could see that the ledge she had now reached was the last deep one visible on the cliff face. The shells in her jersey were restricting her freedom of movement so she decided she would leave them there. Wrapped tight in the towel they would be quite safe. She took the soaking bundle out of her jersey and placed it carefully against the rock face on the ledge beside her, pushing it in as far as it would go. "I'll be back for you," she said, and reached up for the next lip of rock. Just below her the sea crashed against the cliff as if it wanted to suck her from the rock face and claim her once again. Cherry determined not to look down but to concentrate on the climb.

She imagined at first that the glow of light above her was from a torch, and she shouted and screamed until she was weak from the effort of it. But although no answering call came from the night, the light remained, a pale beckoning light whose source now seemed to her wider perhaps than that of a torch. With renewed hope that had rekindled her strength and her courage, Cherry inched her way up the cliff towards the light until she found herself at the entrance to a narrow cave that was filled with a flickering yellow light like that of a candle shaken by the wind. She hauled herself up into the mouth of the cave and sat down exhausted, looking back down at the furious sea frothing beneath her. Relief and joy surged within her and she laughed aloud in triumph. She was safe and she had defied the sea and won. Her one regret was that she had had to leave her cowrie shells behind on the ledge. They were high enough, she thought, to escape the sea. She would fetch them tomorrow after the tide had gone down again.

For the first time now she began to think of her family and how worried they would be, but the thought of walking in through the front door all dripping and dramatic made her almost choke with excitement.

As she reached forward to brush a sharp stone from the sole of her foot, Cherry noticed that the narrow entrance to the cave was half sealed in. She ran her fingers over the stones and cement to make sure, for the light was poor. It was at that moment that she recognized exactly where she was. She recalled now the giant fledgling cuckoo one of her brothers had spotted, being fed by a tiny rock pipit earlier in the holidays, how they had quarrelled over the binoculars and how when she had finally usurped them and made her escape across the rocks she had found the cuckoo perched at the entrance to a narrow cave some way up the cliff face from the beach. She had asked then about the man-made walling and her father had told her of the old tin mines whose lodes and adits criss-crossed the entire coastal area around Zennor. This one, he said, might have been the mine they called Wheel North Grylls, and he thought the adit must have been walled up to prevent the seas from entering the mine in a storm. It was said there had been an accident in the mine only a few years after it was opened over a hundred years before and that the mine had had to close soon after when the mineowners ran out of money to make the necessary repairs. The entire story came back to her now, and she wondered where the cuckoo was and whether the rock pipit had died with the effort of keeping the fledgling alive. Tin mines, she thought, lead to the surface, and the way home. That thought and her natural inquisitiveness about the source of light persuaded her to her feet and into the tunnel.

The adit became narrower and lower as she crept forward, so that she had to go down on her hands and knees and sometimes flat on her stomach. Although she was not out of the wind, it seemed colder. She felt she was moving downwards for a minute or two, for the blood was coming to her head and her weight was heavy on her hands. Then quite suddenly she found the ground levelling out and saw a large tunnel ahead of her. There was no doubt as to which way she should turn for one way the tunnel was black and the other way was lighted with candles that lined the lode wall as far as she could see. She called out aloud: "Anyone there? Anyone there?" and paused to listen for the reply; but all she could hear now was the muffled roar of the sea and the continuous echoing of the dripping water.

The tunnel widened now and she could walk upright again; but her feet hurt against the stone and so she moved slowly, feeling her way gently with each foot. She had gone only a short distance when she heard the tapping for the first time, distinct and rhythmic, a sound that was instantly recognizable as hammering. It became sharper and noticeably more metallic as she moved up the tunnel. She could hear the distant murmur of voices and the sound of falling stone. Before she came out of the tunnel and into the vast cave she knew she had happened upon a working mine.

The cave was dark in all but one corner and here she could see two men bending to their work, their backs towards her. One of them was inspecting the rock face closely whilst the other swung his hammer with controlled power, pausing only to spit on his hands from time to time. They wore round hats with turned-up brims that served also as candlesticks, for a lighted candle was fixed to each, the light dancing with the shadows along the cave walls as they worked.

Cherry watched for some moments until she made up her mind what to do. She longed to rush up to them and tell of her escape and to ask them to take her to the surface, but a certain shyness overcame her and she held back. Her chance to interrupt came when they sat down against the rock face and opened their canteen. She was in the shadows and they still could not see her.

"Tea looks cold again," one of them said gruffly. "'Tis always cold, I'm sure she makes it wi' cold water."

"Oh stop your moaning, Father," said the other, a younger voice, Cherry felt. "She does her best. She's five little ones to look after and precious little to do it on. She does her best. You mustn't keep on at her so. It upsets her. She does her best."

"So she does, lad, so she does. And so for that matter, do I, but that don't stop her moaning at me and it'll not stop me moaning at her. If we didn't moan at each other, lad, we'd have precious little else to talk about, and that's a fact. She expects it of me, lad, and I expects it of her."

"Excuse me," Cherry said tentatively. She felt she had eavesdropped for long enough. She approached them slowly. "Excuse me, but I've got a bit lost. I climbed the cliff, you see, 'cos I was cut off from the Cove. I was trying to get back, but I couldn't and I saw this light and so I climbed up. I want to get home and I wondered if you could help me get to the top?"

"Top?" said the older one, peering into the dark. "Come closer, lad, where we can see you."

"She's not a lad, Father. Are you blind? Can you not see 'tis a filly. 'Tis a young filly, all wet through from the sea. Come," the young man said, standing up and beckoning Cherry in. "Don't be afeared little girl, we shan't harm you. Come on, you can have some of my tea if you like."

They spoke their words in a manner Cherry had never heard before. It was not the usual Cornish burr, but heavier and rougher in tone and somehow old-fashioned. There were so many questions in her mind.

"But I thought the mine was closed a hundred years ago," she said nervously. "That's what I was told anyway."

"Well, you was told wrong," said the old man whom Cherry could see more clearly now under his candle. His eyes were white and set far back in his head, unnaturally so she thought, and his lips and mouth seemed a vivid red in the candlelight.

"Closed, closed indeed, does it look closed to you? D'you think we're digging for worms? Over four thousand tons of tin last year and nine thousand of copper ore, and you ask is the mine closed! Over twenty fathoms below the sea this mine goes. We'll dig right out under the ocean, most of the way to 'Merica afore we close down this mine."

He spoke passionately now, almost angrily, so that Cherry felt she had offended him.

"Hush, Father," said the young man, taking off his jacket and wrapping it around Cherry's shoulders. "She doesn't want to hear all about that. She's cold and wet. Can't you see? Now let's make a little fire to warm her through. She's shivered right through to her bones. You can see she is."

"They all are," said the old timer, pulling himself to his feet. "They all are." And he shuffled past her into the dark. "I'll fetch the wood," he muttered, and then added, "for all the good it'll do."

"What does he mean?" Cherry asked the young man, for whom she felt an instant liking. "What did he mean by that?"

"Oh pay him no heed, little girl," he said. "He's an old man now and tired of the mine. We're both tired of it, but we're proud of it see, and we've nowhere else to go, nothing else to do."

He had a kind voice that was reassuring to Cherry. He seemed somehow to know the questions she wanted to ask, for he answered them now without her ever asking.

"Sit down by me while you listen, girl," he said. "Father will make a fire to warm you and I shall tell you how we come to be here. You won't be afeared now, will you?"

Cherry looked up into his face which was younger than she had expected from his voice; but like his father's the eyes seemed sad and deep set, yet they smiled at her gently and she smiled back.

"That's my girl. It was a new mine this, promising everyone said. The best tin in Cornwall and that means the best tin in the world. 1865 it started up and they were looking for tinners, and so Father found a cottage down by Treveal and came to work here. I was already fourteen, so I joined him down the mine. We prospered and the mine prospered, to start with. Mother and the little children had full bellies and there was talk of sinking a fresh shaft. Times were good and promised to be better."

Cherry sat transfixed as the story of the disaster unfolded. She heard how they had been trapped by a fall of rocks, about how they had worked to pull them away, but behind every rock was another rock and another rock. She heard how they had never even heard any sound of rescue. They had died, he said, in two days or so because the air was bad and because there was too little of it.

"Father has never accepted it; he still thinks he's alive, that he goes home to Mother and the little children each evening. But he's dead, just like me. I can't tell him though, for he'd not understand and it would break his heart if he ever knew."

"So you aren't real," said Cherry, trying to grasp the implications of his story. "So I'm just imagining all this. You're just a dream?"

"No dream, my girl," said the young man laughing out loud. "No more'n we're imagining you. We're real right enough, but we're dead and have been for a hundred years and more. Ghosts, spirits, that's what living folk call us, come to think of it that's what I called us when I was alive."

Cherry was on her feet suddenly and backing away.

"No need to be afeared, little girl," said the young man, holding out his hand towards her. "We won't harm you. No one can harm you, not now. Look, he's started the fire already. Come over and warm yourself. Come, it'll be all right, girl. We'll look after you. We'll help you."

"But I want to go home," Cherry said, feeling the

panic rising to her voice and trying to control it. "I know you're kind, but I want to go home. My mother will be worried about me. They'll be out looking for me. Your light saved my life and I want to thank you. But I must go else they'll worry themselves sick, I know they will."

"You going back home?" the young man asked, and then he nodded. "I s'pose you'll want to see your family again."

"'Course I am," said Cherry, perplexed by the question. " 'Course I do."

" 'Tis a pity," he said sadly. "Everyone passes through and no one stays. They all want to go home, but then so do I. You'll want me to guide you to the surface I s'pose."

"I'm not the first then?" Cherry said. "There's been others climb up into the mine to escape from the sea? You saved lots of people then?"

"A few," said the tinner, nodding. "A few."

"You're a kind person," Cherry said, warming to the sadness in the young man's voice. "I never thought ghosts would be kind."

"We're just people, people who've passed on," replied the young man, taking her elbow and leading her towards the fire. "There's nice people and there's nasty people. It's the same if you're alive or if you're dead. You're a nice person, I can tell that, even though I haven't known you for long. I'm sad because I should like to be alive again with my friends and go rabbiting or blackberrying up by the chapel near Treveal like I used to. The sun always seemed to be shining then. After it happened I used to go up to the surface often and move amongst the people in the village. I went to see my family, but if I spoke to them they never seemed to hear me and of course they can't see you. You can see them, but they can't see you. That's the worst of it. So I don't go up much now, just to collect wood for the fire and a bit of food now and then. I stay down here with Father in the mine and we work away day after day, and from time to time someone like you comes up the tunnel from the sea and lightens our darkness. I shall be sad when you go."

The old man was hunched over the fire rubbing his hands and holding them out over the heat.

"Not often we have a fire," he said, his voice more sprightly now. "Only on special occasions. Birthdays of course, we always have a fire on birthdays back at the cottage. Martha's next. You don't know her; she's my only daughter – she'll be eight on September 10th. She's been poorly you know – her lungs, that's what the doctor said." He sighed deeply. " 'Tis dreadful damp in the cottage. 'Tis well nigh impossible to keep it out." There was a tremor in the old man's voice that betrayed his emotion. He looked up at

Cherry and she could see the tears in his eyes. "She looks a bit like you, my dear, raven-haired and as pretty as a picture; but not so tall, not so tall. Come in closer, my dear, you'll be warmer that way."

Cherry sat with them by the fire till it died away to nothing. She longed to go, to get home amongst the living, but the old man talked on of his family and their little one-room cottage with a ladder to the bedroom where they all huddled together for warmth, of his friends that used to meet in the Tinners' Arms every evening. There were tales of wrecking and smuggling, and all the while the young man sat silent until there was a lull in the story.

"Father," he said. "I think our little friend would like to go home now. Shall I take her up as I usually do?" The old man nodded and waved his hand in dismissal.

"Come back and see us sometime, if you've a mind to," he said, and then put his face in his hands.

"Goodbye," said Cherry. "Thank you for the fire and for helping me. I won't forget you." But the old man never replied.

The journey through the mine was long and difficult. She held fast to the young tinner's waist as they walked silently through the dark tunnels, stopping every now and then to climb a ladder to the lode above until finally they could look up the shaft

above them and see the daylight shining in the sky.

"It's dawn," said the young man, looking up.

"I'll be back in time for breakfast," said Cherry, setting her foot on the ladder.

"You'll remember me?" the young tinner asked, and Cherry nodded, unable to speak. She felt a strange affinity with him and his father. "And if you should ever need me, come back again. You may need me and I shall be here. I go nowhere else."

"Thank you," said Cherry. "I won't forget. I doubt anyone is going to believe me when I tell them about you. No one believes in ghosts, not up there."

"I doubt it too. Be happy, little friend," he said. And he was gone, back into the tunnel. Cherry waited until the light from the candle in his hat had vanished and then turned eagerly to the ladder and began to climb up towards the light.

She found herself in a place she knew well, high on the moor by Zennor Quoit. She stood by the ruined mine workings and looked down at the sleeping village shrouded in mist, and the calm blue sea beyond. The storm had passed and there was scarcely a breath of wind even on the moor. It was only ten minutes' walk down through the bracken, across the road by the Eagle's Nest and down the farm track to the cottage where her family would be waiting. She began to run, but the clothes were still heavy and wet and she was soon reduced to a fast walk. All the while she was determining where she would begin her story, wondering how much they would believe. At the top of the lane she stopped to consider how best to make her entrance. Should she ring the bell and be found standing there, or should she just walk in and surprise them there at breakfast? She longed to see the joy on their faces, to feel the warmth of their arms around her and to bask once again in their affection.

She saw as she came round the corner by the cottage that there was a long blue Land Rover parked in the lane bristling with aerials. "Coastguard" she read on the side. As she came down the steps she noticed that the back door of the cottage was open and she could hear voices inside. She stole in on tiptoe. The kitchen was full of uniformed men drinking tea and around the table sat her family, dejection and despair etched on every face. They hadn't seen her yet. One of the uniformed men had put down his cup and was speaking. His voice was low and hushed.

"You're sure the towel is hers, no doubts about it?"

Cherry's mother shook her head.

"It's her towel," she said quietly, "and they are her shells. She must have put them up there, must have been the last thing she did."

Cherry saw her shells spread out on the open towel and stifled a shout of joy.

"We have to say," he went on, "we have to say then, most regrettably, that the chances of finding your daughter alive now are very slim. It seems she must have tried to climb the cliff to escape the heavy seas and fallen in. We've scoured the cliff top for miles in both directions and covered the entire beach, and there's no sign of her. She must have been washed out to sea. We must conclude that she is missing, and we have to presume that she is drowned."

Cherry could listen no longer but burst into the room shouting.

"I'm home, I'm home. Look at me, I'm not drowned

at all. I'm here! I'm home!"

The tears were running down her face.

But no one in the room even turned to look in her direction. Her brothers lay on their arms and cried openly, one of them clutching the giant's necklace.

"But it's me," she shouted again. "Me, can't you see? It's me and I've come back. I'm all right. Look at me."

But no one did, and no one heard.

The giant's necklace lay spread out on the table.

"So she'll never finish it after all," said her mother softly. "Poor Cherry. Poor dear Cherry."

And in that one moment Cherry knew and understood that she was right, that she would never finish her necklace, that she belonged no longer with the living but had passed on beyond.

Siren Song

Vivien Alcock

1 August 1981

Dear Tape Recorder,

This is me. My name's Roger and I'm nine years old today. You're my birthday present.

> Happy birthday to me,
> Happy birthday to you,
> Happy birthday, dear both-of-us . . .

1 August 1982

R for Roger. R for Roger. This is Roger, mark ten, calling. I'm not going to bore you with a bite-by-bite account of my birthday tea, like last year. This time I'll only record the exciting moments in my life. Over and out.

1 August 1983

My name is Roger Kent. I am eleven years old. I

want to get this down in case anything happens to me.

I hate this village. I wish we hadn't come to live here. There's something funny about it.

For one thing, there are no other children here. Except Billy Watson, and he's weird. He's a thin, white-faced boy who jumps when you speak to him. Mum says he's been ill, and I must be kind. I was. I asked him to come to my birthday tea today. He twitched like I'd stabbed him in the back, and his eyes scuttled about like beetles. Then he mumbled something and ran off.

The grown-ups are peculiar, too. They're old and baggy-eyed, as if they'd been crying all night. When they see me, they stop talking. They watch me. It's a bit scary.

At first I thought they didn't like me. But it's not that. They look as if they know something terrible's going to happen to me, and are sorry about it.

Mrs Mason's the worst. I hate the way she looks at me. Her eyes are . . . I dunno . . . sort of hungry. I don't mean she's a cannibal. It's more like . . . D'you know why gerbils sometimes eat their own babies? It's because they're afraid they're in danger, and think they'll be safer back inside.

That's just how Mrs Mason looks at me. As if she'd like to swallow me to keep me safe. But what from?

This morning, when she heard it was my birthday, she hugged me. I jerked away. I didn't mean to be rude. I honestly thought she was going to start nibbling my ear. That's the sort of state I'm in.

"Never go out at night," she said. (That's nothing. Mum's always telling me that nowadays. It's what came next.) "Never go out at night, *whatever sounds you hear!*"

Funny thing to say, wasn't it? "Whatever sounds you hear!"

I've been thinking and thinking, but I can't imagine what she meant. If we lived by the sea, I'd think of smugglers. You know, like that poem – "Watch the wall, my darling, while the gentlemen go by."

Perhaps they're witches! I'm not being silly. There *are* witches nowadays. It was in the papers once. COVEN OF WITCHES EXPOSED, it said. They certainly were exposed! There was this photograph of men and women with nothing on. Not that you could see much, only their backs. They didn't look wild and exciting at all. Just stupid. And cold – you could almost see the goosepimples. Still, they were witches.

D'you think it's that?

Full moon tonight. I'm going to stay awake and listen. It must be happening somewhere near enough for me to hear, or she wouldn't have said that.

Supposing they use our garden?

Suppose Mum's joined them! She's been a bit strange lately. No, that's silly.

10.30 p.m. I'm sitting by the window. Nothing's happened yet. Just the usual night noises, and not many of those. This village dies after ten o'clock. A dog barking. An owl getting on my nerves, can't the stupid thing say anything else?

It's boring. I think I'll go to bed for a bit.

0.00. I've got a digital clock and that's what it say. Like Time's laid eggs in a row. No time. Nothing point nothing nothing time. Don't count your minutes before they're hatched.

What's that?

Only an owl. The window's wide open, and it's cold. The moon is round and bright. There are shadows all over the garden. I can't see anything. It's very quiet now. No wind.

Listen!

Children! I can hear children laughing. I can hear their voices calling softly . . .

I think they're in Billy Watson's garden. He must be having a midnight party, and he hasn't asked me!

Pig! No wonder he ran off when I invited him to tea.

I wish I could see them. There're too many trees. Too many shadows.

Listen!

The microphone's too small. I held it out of the window, but I didn't get anything.

They were singing. Their voices were high and clear. I could hear every word. It was a funny little tune. Sort of sad, but nice. There's a chorus where they all hoot softly like baby owls. I think I can remember the words –

> "Little ghost, all dressed in white,
> Walking on a summer's night,
> (Hooo, hooo,)
> Calling to her childhood friend,
> Asking him to come and play,
> But his hair stands up on end.
> Billy Watson runs away."

Billy Watson! So they are friends of his! I suppose they're playing a game . . .

Listen . . .

It was a girl singing alone this time. I'm sure it was a girl. Her voice was so high and sweet and sad, it made me ache. This is what she sang –

"Don't you love me any more?
I'm as pretty as before.
(Hooo, hooo,)
Though my roses all are gone,
Lily-white is just as sweet.
Stars shine through me now, not on
Flesh that's only so much meat."

I wish I could see her . . .

"Coo-ee! Over here!"

They heard me. I know they did. They're whispering. Now they're coming nearer. I can hear the bushes rustling by our wall. Look! I think one of them's slipped over into our garden. It's difficult to be sure. There are so many shadows. I'm going to dangle the microphone out of the window . . .

Listen!

"Billy, see the moon is bright.
Won't you play with me tonight?
(Hooo, hooo,)
Billy Watson's now in bed,
With his fingers in his ears,
And his blankets hide his head,
And his face is wet with tears."

I got it that time! It's very faint, but you can just make out the words. I don't think they can be friends of Billy's after all. They sounded as if they were mocking him. I wonder who they are?

Oh, they're going away now! I can hear them running through the bushes. Laughing. They've gone!

No, there's still one standing in the shadow of the lilac tree. Just below my window. I'm sure it's the girl. I can see her white frock gleaming ... unless it's just the moonlight. She's all alone now. Waiting for me.

Listen!

"Little ghost all dressed in white
Singing sadly in the night,
(Hooo, hooo,)
Who will play with me instead?
Must I be lonely till the end?
Is there any child abed,
Brave enough to be my friend?"

I'm coming! Wait for me! I know I promised Mum I'd never go out at night, but . . . The moon is shining bright as day. Someone is singing in the garden below. Softly. Sweetly. Surely it won't matter if I go out just once?

The rest of the tape is blank. Roger Kent was never seen again.

The Spring

Peter Dickinson

When Derek was seven Great-Aunt Tessa had died and there'd been a funeral party for all the relations. In the middle of it a woman with a face like a sick fish, some kind of cousin, had grabbed hold of Derek and half-talked to him and half-talked to another cousin over his head.

"That's a handsome young fellow, aren't you? (Just like poor old Charlie, that age.) So you're young Derek. How old would you be now, then? (The girls – that's one of them, there, in the green blouse – they're a lot bigger.) Bit of an afterthought, weren't you, Derek? Nice surprise for your mum and dad. (Meg had been meaning to go back to that job of hers, you know . . .)"

And so on, just as if she'd been talking two languages, one he could understand and one he couldn't. Derek hadn't been surprised or shocked. In his heart he'd known all along.

It wasn't that anyone was unkind to him, or even uncaring. Of course his sisters sometimes called him a pest and told him to go away, but mostly the family included him in whatever they were doing and sometimes, not just on his birthday, did something they thought would amuse him. But even those times Derek knew in his heart that he wasn't really meant to be there. If he'd never been born – well, like the cousin said, Mum would have gone back to her job full-time, and five years earlier too, and she'd probably have got promoted so there'd have been more money for things. And better holidays sooner. And more room in the house – Cindy was always whining about having to share with Fran . . . It's funny to think about a world in which you've never existed, never been born. It would seem almost exactly the same to everyone else. They wouldn't miss you – there'd never have been anything for them to miss.

About four years after Great-Aunt Tessa's funeral Dad got a new job and the family moved south. That June Dad and Mum took Derek off to look at a lot of roses. They had their new garden to fill, and there was this famous collection of roses only nine miles away at Something Abbey, so they could go and see if there were ones they specially liked, and get their order in for next winter. Mum and Dad were nuts about gardens. The girls had ploys of their own but it was a tagging-along afternoon for Derek.

The roses grew in a big walled garden, hundreds and hundreds of them, all different, with labels. Mum and Dad stood in front of each bush in turn, cocking their heads and pursing their lips while they decided if they liked it. They'd smell a bloom or two, and then Mum would read the label and Dad would look it up in his book to see if it was disease-resistant; last of all, Mum might write its name in her notebook and they'd give it marks, out of six, like skating-judges, and move on. It took *hours*.

After a bit Mum remembered about Derek.

"Why don't you go down to the house and look at the river, darling? Don't fall in."

"Got your watch?" said Dad. "OK, back at the car park, four-fifteen sharp."

He gave Derek a pound in case there were ice creams anywhere and turned back to the roses.

The river was better than the roses, a bit. The lawn of the big house ran down and became its bank. It was as wide as a road, not very deep but clear with dark green weed streaming in the current and trout sometimes darting between. Derek found a twig and chucked it in, pacing beside it and timing its speed on his watch. He counted trout for a while, and then walking further along the river he came to a strange shallow stream which ran through the lawns, like a winding path, only water, just a few inches deep but rushing through its channel in quick ripples. Following it up he came to a sort of hole in the ground, with a fence round it. The hole had stone sides and was full of water. The water came rushing up from somewhere underground, almost as though it were boiling. It was very clear. You could see a long way down.

While Derek stood staring, a group of other visitors strolled up and one of them started reading from her guidebook, gabbling and missing bits out.

". . . remarkable spring . . . pre-dates all the rest of the abbey . . . no doubt why the monks settled here . . . white chalk bowl fifteen feet across and twelve feet deep . . . crystal-clear water surges out at about two hundred gallons a minute . . . always the same temperature, summer and winter . . ."

"Magical, don't you think?" said another of the tourists.

She didn't mean it. "Magical" was just a word to her.

But yes, Derek thought, magical. Where does it come from? So close to the river, too, but it's got nothing to do with that. Perhaps it comes from another world.

He thought he'd only stood gazing for a short time, hypnotized by the rush of water welling and welling out of nowhere, but when he looked at his watch, it was ten past four. There was an ice-cream van, but Dad and Mum didn't get back to the car till almost twenty to five.

That night Derek dreamt about the spring. Nothing much happened in the dream, only he was standing beside it, looking down. It was night-time, with a full moon, and he was waiting for the moon to be reflected from the rumpled water. Something would happen then. He woke before it happened, with his heart hammering. He was filled with a sort of dread, though the dream hadn't been a nightmare. The dread was sort of neutral, halfway between terror and glorious excitement.

The same dream happened the next night, and the next, and the next. When it woke him on the fifth night, he thought, This is getting to be a nuisance.

He got out of bed and went to the window. It was a brilliant night, with a full moon high. He felt wide awake. He turned from the window, meaning to get back into bed, but somehow found himself moving into his getting-up routine, taking his pyjamas off and pulling on his shirt. The moment he realized what he was doing he stopped himself, but then thought, Why not? It'd fix that dream, at least. He laughed silently to himself and finished dressing. Ten minutes later he was bicycling through the dark.

Derek knew the way to the abbey because Mum was no use at map reading so that was something he did on car journeys – a way of joining in. He thought he could do it in an hour and a quarter, so he'd be there a bit after one. He'd be pretty tired by the time he got back, but the roads were flat down here compared with Yorkshire. He'd left a note on the kitchen table saying: "Gone for a ride. Back for breakfast." They'd think he'd just gone out for an early-morning spin – he was always first up. Nine miles there and nine back made eighteen. He'd done fifteen in one go last month. Shouldn't be too bad.

And in fact, although the night was still, he rode as though there was a stiff breeze at his back, hardly getting tired at all. Late cars swished through the dark. He tried to think of a story in case anyone stopped and asked what he was doing – if a police car came by it certainly would – but no one did. He reached the abbey at ten past one. The gate was shut, of course. He hadn't even thought about getting in. There might be ivy, or something.

He found some, a bit back along the way he'd come, but it wasn't strong or thick enough to climb. Still, it didn't cross his mind that he wouldn't get in. He was going to. There would be a way.

The wall turned away from the road beside the garden of another house. Derek wheeled his bike through the gate and pushed it in among some bushes, then followed the wall back through the garden. No light shone from the house. Nobody stirred. He followed the wall of the abbey grounds along towards the back of the garden. He thought he could hear the river rustling beyond. The moonlight was very bright, casting shadows so black they looked solid. The garden became an orchard, heavy old trees, their leafy branches blotting out the moon, but with a clear space further on. Ducking beneath the branches, he headed towards it. The night air smelt of something new, sweetish, familiar – fresh-cut sawdust. When he reached the clear space, he found it surrounded a tree trunk which had had all its branches cut off and just stood there like a twisted arm sticking out of the ground. Leaning against it was a ladder.

It wasn't very heavy. Derek carried it over to the abbey wall. It reached almost to the top. He climbed, straddled the wall, leaned down and with an effort hauled the ladder up and lowered it on the further side, down into the darkness under the trees that grew there, then climbed down and groped his way out towards where the moonlight gleamed between the tree trunks. Out in the open on the upper slope of lawn he got his bearings, checked for a landmark so that he would be able to find his way back to the ladder, and walked down in the shadow of the trees towards the river. His heart was beginning to thump, the way it did in the dream. The same dread, between terror and glory, seemed to bubble up inside him.

When he was level with the spring he walked across the open and stood by the low fence, gazing down at the troubled water. It looked very black, and in this light he couldn't see into it at all. He tried to find the exact place he had stood in the dream, and waited. A narrow rim of moon-shadow cast by the wall on the left side edged the disc of water below. It thinned and thinned as the slow-moving moon heeled west. And now it was gone.

The reflection of the moon, broken and scattered by the endlessly upswelling water, began to pass glimmeringly across the disc below. Derek could feel the turn of the world making it move like that. His heartbeat came in hard pulses, seeming to shake his body. Without knowing what he was doing, he climbed the fence and clung to its inner side so that he could gaze straight down into the water. His own reflection, broken by the ripples, was a squat black shape against the silver moonlight. He crouched with his left arm clutching the lowest rail and with his right arm strained down towards it. He could just reach. The black shape changed as the reflection of his arm came to meet it. The water was only water to his touch.

Somehow he found another few centimetres of stretch and plunged his hand through the surface. The water was still water, but then another hand gripped his.

He almost lost his balance and fell, but the other hand didn't try to pull him in. It didn't let go either. When Derek tried to pull free the hand came with him, and an arm behind it. He pulled, heaved, strained. A head broke the surface. Another arm reached up and gripped the top of the side wall. Now

Derek could straighten and take a fresh hold higher up the fence. And now the stranger could climb out, gasping and panting, over the fence, and stand on the moonlit lawn beside him. He was a boy about Derek's own age, wearing ordinary clothes like Derek's. They were dry to the touch.

"I thought you weren't coming," said the boy. "Have we got somewhere to live?"

"I suppose you'd better come home."

They walked together towards the trees.

"Who . . .?" began Derek.

"Not now," said the stranger.

They stole on in silence. We'll have to walk the whole way home, thought Derek. Mightn't get in before breakfast. How'm I going to explain?

The ladder was still against the wall. They climbed it, straddled the top, lowered the ladder the far side and climbed down, propping it back against its tree. Then back towards the road.

There were two bikes hidden in the bushes.

"How on . . .?" began Derek.

"Not now," said the stranger.

They biked in silence the whole way home, getting in just as the sky was turning grey. They took off their shoes and tiptoed up the stairs. Derek was so tired he couldn't remember going to bed.

*

They were woken by Cindy's call outside the door.

"Hi! Pests! Get up! School bus in twenty mins!"

Derek scrambled into his clothes and just beat David down the stairs. Dad was in the hallway, looking through the post before driving off to work.

"Morning, twins," he said. "Decided to have a lie-in?"

They gobbled their breakfast and caught the bus by running. Jimmy Grove had kept two seats for them. He always did.

Very occasionally during that year Derek felt strange. There was something not quite right in the world, something out of balance, some shadow. It was like that feeling you have when you think you've glimpsed something out of the corner of your eye but when you turn your head it isn't there. Once or twice it was so strong he almost said something. One evening, for instance, he and David were sitting either side of Mum while she leafed through an old photograph album. They laughed or groaned at pictures of themselves as babies, or in fancy dress – Tweedledum and Tweedledee – and then Mum pointed at a picture of an old woman with a crooked grinning face, like a jolly witch, and said, "I don't suppose you remember her. That's Great-Aunt Tessa. You went to her funeral."

"I remember the funeral," said David. "There was a grisly sort of cousin who grabbed us and told us how handsome we were, and then talked over our heads about us to someone else as if we couldn't understand what she was saying."

"She had a face like a sick fish," said Derek.

"Oh, Cousin Vi. She's a pain in the neck. She . . ."

And Mum rattled on about Cousin Vi's murky doings for a bit and then turned the page, but for a moment Derek felt that he had almost grasped the missing whatever-it-was, almost turned his head quick enough to see something before it vanished. No.

On the whole it was a pretty good year. There were dud bits. David broke a leg in the Christmas hols, which spoilt things for a while. The girls kept complaining that the house wasn't big enough for seven, especially with the pests growing so fast, but then Jackie got a job and went to live with friends in a flat in Totton. Dad bought a new car. Those were the most exciting things that happened, so it was a nothing-much year, but not bad. And then one weekend in June Mum and Dad went off to the abbey to look at the roses again. Cindy and Fran were seeing friends, so it was just the twins who tagged along.

The roses were the same as last year, and Mum and

Dad slower than ever, so after a bit David said, "Let's go and look at the river. OK, Mum?"

Dad gave them a quid each for ices and told them when to be back at the car. They raced twigs on the river, tried to spot the largest trout, and then found the stream that ran through the lawn and followed it up to the spring. They stood staring at the uprushing water for a long while, not saying anything. In the end, Derek looked at his watch, saw it was almost four, woke David from his trance and raced him off to look for ices.

A few nights later Derek woke with his heart pounding. It was something he'd dreamt, but he couldn't remember the dream. He sat up and saw that David's bed was empty. When he got up and put his hand between the sheets, they were still just warm to the touch.

All at once memory came back, the eleven years when he'd been on his own and the year when he'd had David. The other years, the ones when he'd been growing up with a twin brother and the photographs in the album had been taken – they weren't real. By morning he wouldn't remember them. By morning he wouldn't remember David either. There was just this one night.

He rushed into his clothes, crept down the stairs

and out. The door was unlocked. David's bike was already gone from the shed. He got his own out and started off.

The night was still, but he felt as though he had an intangible wind in his face. Every pedal-stroke was an effort. He put his head down and rode on. Normally, he knew, he'd be faster than David, whose leg still wasn't properly strong after his accident, but tonight he guessed David would have the spirit wind behind him, the wind from some other world. Derek didn't think he would catch him. All he knew was that he had to try.

In fact he almost ran into him, about two miles from the abbey, just after the turn off the main road. David was trotting along beside his bike, pushing it, gasping for breath.

"What's happened?" said Derek.

"Got a puncture. Lend me yours. I'll be too late."

"Get up behind. We'll need us both to climb the wall. There mayn't be a ladder this time."

Without a word David climbed on to the saddle. Derek stood on the pedals and drove the bike on through the dark. They leaned the bike against the wall where the ivy grew. It still wasn't thick enough to climb, but it was something to get a bit of a grip on. David stood on the saddle of the bike. Derek put his hands under his heels and heaved him up, grunting with the effort, till David could grip the coping of the wall. He still couldn't pull himself right up, but he found a bit of a foothold in the ivy and hung there while Derek climbed on to the crossbar, steadied himself and let David use his shoulder as a step. A heave, a scrabble, and he was on the wall.

Derek stood on the saddle and reached up. He couldn't look, but felt David reach down to touch his hand, perhaps just to say goodbye. Derek gripped the hand and held. David heaved. Scrabbling and stretching, Derek leaped for the coping. He heard the bike clatter away beneath him. David's other hand grabbed his collar. He had an elbow on the coping,

and now a knee, and he was up.

"Thanks," he muttered.

The drop on the far side was into blackness. There could have been anything below, but there seemed no help for it. You just had to hang from the coping, let go and trust to luck. Derek landed on softness but wasn't ready for the impact and stumbled, banging his head against the wall. He sat down, his whole skull filled with the pain of it. Dimly he heard a sort of crash, and as the pain seeped away worked out that David must have fallen into a bush. More cracks and rustles as David struggled free.

"Are you OK?" came his voice.

"Think so. Hit my head."

"Where are you?"

"I'm OK. Let's get on."

They struggled out through a sort of shrubbery, making enough noise, it seemed, to wake all Hampshire. Derek's head was just sore on the outside now. Blood was running down his cheek. David was already running, a dark limping shape about twenty metres away. His leg must have gone duff again after all that effort. Derek followed him across the moonlit slopes and levels. They made no effort to hide. If anyone had been watching from the house they must have seen them, the moonlight was so strong. At last they stood panting by the fence of the spring. The rim of shadow still made a thin line under a wall.

"Done it," whispered David. "I thought I was stuck."

"What'd have happened?"

"Don't know."

"What's it like . . . the other side?"

"Different. Shh."

The shadow vanished and the reflection of the moon on to the troubled disc. Derek glanced sideways at his brother's face. The rippled, reflected light glimmered across it, making it very strange, grey-white like a mushroom, and changing all the time as the ripples changed, as if it wasn't even sure of its own proper shape.

David climbed the fence, grasped the bottom rail and lowered his legs into the water. Derek climbed too, gripped David's hand and crouched to lower his brother – yes, his brother still – his last yard in this world. David let go of the rail and dropped. Derek gripped his hand all the way to the water.

As he felt that silvery touch the movement stopped, and they hung there, either side of the rippled mirror. David didn't seem to want to let go, either.

Different? thought Derek. Different how?

The hand wriggled, impatient. Something must be

happening the other side. No time to make up his mind. He let go of the rail.

In the instant that he plunged towards the water he felt a sort of movement around him, very slight, but clear. It was the whole world closing in, filling the gap where he had been. In that instant, he realized, everything changed. Jackie would still be at home, Fran would be asleep in his room, not needing to share with Cindy. Nobody would shout at him to come to breakfast. His parents would go about their day with no sense of loss; Jimmy Grove would keep no place for him on the school bus; Mum would be a director of her company, with a car of her own . . . and all the photographs in the albums would show the same cheerful family, two parents, three daughters, no gap, not even the faintest shadow that might once have been Derek.

He was leaving a world where he had never been born.

The Coming of the Wolf

Annie Dalton

For days Jacob Owen had known the wolf was there. He just avoided meeting it face to face, believing no one in his right mind would choose to be haunted by a wolf, particularly one who, like a wolf in a glass snowstorm, brought his own blizzard with him.

It started gradually; a little whining and scratching under the window at dawn, then the appearance of a pair of huge yellow eyes at the end of the garden like reproachful foglamps before Jake drew the curtain at night. Easy to explain away. There are always strays, even on a smart estate like Hither Green.

But when he woke one Saturday when it was barely light, to gigantic frosty paw prints melting on the summer lawn, he knew he was in serious trouble.

As he stole down uncarpeted stairs he saw the back door was already open. Lizzy, his twin, was waiting under the cherry tree. She made room for him without surprise.

"There was a dog howling," she said, shivering. "I couldn't sleep."

Jake looked around nervously but the wolf prints had vanished, leaving only a chill in the air.

It was the loneliness of the wolf business that was so hard, coming as it did on top of the move from the old friendly house, their mother's marriage to Derek. Max. (Jake felt a sinking feeling just thinking about his stepbrother Max.)

Only a few weeks ago he could have told Lizzy and she would have made it part of the shared magic of the Game and the dread would have drained out of it. But the Game belonged to the old Jake and Lizzy and he was afraid they were gone forever.

"At least you don't have to share that poky room," he said savagely. "I can hear him breathing even when I'm asleep. I hate Max Harris. I hate his slimy hair gel and I hate his smelly breath."

The part he couldn't say was how scary it felt listening in the dark to the eerie whale music Max made through chronically blocked sinuses all night long. It was the loneliest sound in the world.

Later in the day Lizzy might pretend she didn't

understand. Newly awake under the cherry tree she was still his twin sister. His other self.

"It's so cramped upstairs you can hear *everyone* breathing," she said.

"You can hear the man next door go to the loo," said Jake. They grinned.

"But it's only a stopgap house. Until the new one's ready."

Jake didn't answer. Ever since they'd arrived at Hither Green he'd felt like an underwater swimmer, holding his breath, unable to get back to the old life, not sure he even wanted to reach the strange far-off shores of the new.

Lizzy and Jake weren't identical. If anything they were opposites. Lizzy was all skin and bone, all dash and sparkle like a shooting star. Her thoughts zoomed round her head at the speed of light. If she was a flower she'd be a morning glory; an explosion of blue. Jake was a background person, a woodland honeysuckle. His thoughts grew slowly and secretly like the rings round trees.

No one could ever see why they got on. Jake didn't care. He just knew that when he was around Lizzy, not just the world, but his own body felt more solid, more trustworthy. With Lizzy he was complete. A puzzle that had come out right.

But lately Jake felt increasingly like a lonely

question no one could answer. A ghostly hologram anyone could walk through. It had something to do with the stopgap house and everything to do with Lizzy, who was drifting gently a little further away from him each day, like a kite with a fraying string.

"Mum's happy," said Lizzy. Her hair had almost grown back. Lizzy had hacked it off with the kitchen scissors for Children of War. Mum just laughed and swept up the hair but Derek was appalled. Jake could tell he thought he'd come into their lives just in time.

"And the new house will be brilliant," said Lizzy. "Tons of room for everyone to breathe as much as they want."

"I liked being a twin," said Jake.

"You still are a twin, idiot. Once a twin always a twin." Lizzy wound an arm around him, bumping her head against his, less gently than she might have done, her usual mixed message of warning and affection. She might be his twin but she was Ruth's daughter first and Ruth believed so hard in happy families, happy endings, she'd do anything she had to to get one.

"No," he said, shaking his head. "They want to make me into a boy like Max. Collections and computer games. The Harrises want to swallow the Owens up. What I really hate is how they won't even let us keep our *name*."

Jake believed in happy endings too. He was sure he did. But the true kind, where everyone had their fair say. Not the pretend kind where one family gobbled another up like cannibals.

"Why do you care so much?" asked Lizzy irritably. She was drifting away again, Jake saw. Her magic Owen self fading like the moon. Her Harris self rising high and pitiless. Harrises believed in facts and answers.

"I mean he left you, Jacob Owen. Why do you want to keep his stupid name? It really makes things hard for Mum."

"I know Dad left me," said Jake, careful not to say their dad had left Lizzy too. "But I didn't leave him, you see."

Lizzy avoided his gaze and then said, scrambling up, very bright so that Jake couldn't tell for sure if she was Harris or Owen, Sun or Moon, "When it's properly tomorrow we could start a new Game if you want."

"I don't think we could play it here."

Neither he nor Lizzy had even mentioned the Game since they moved to the new house. It was part of the distance growing between them.

Lizzy drew herself taller. "We can play the Game wherever we are," she said using her spellbinding

Game voice. They had a rule. Whatever Lizzy said in that voice was true. In this mood she was all Lizzy Owen; soaked in moonlight and magic to her toenails. But still Jake worried and grumbled.

"If we play it here," he called after her, "Max will have to play too, won't he?"

"Maybe," she said enigmatically. "But he probably won't want to."

"And the house is too small."

"We could play in the garage," Lizzy called. "That's huge."

Then she vanished, leaving Jake wondering if it wasn't a kind of betrayal to start the Game up again under the knowing green eyes of their stepbrother Max.

The next moment he was bowled off his feet by a blast of freezing air and a flurry of snow. Not flakes but the stinging gritty stuff that comes in late winter, littering gutters like oatmeal. Winter snow.

Dazed, sure he must be dreaming after all, he staggered lopsidedly into the storm, until he reached the street. His eyes widened in shock.

Someone had punched or torn a hole in the world and it was through the cloudy frame of this terrifying space that the harsh winter wind was blowing.

The wolf was on the other side of the frame, eyes burning in the half-light of almost dawn.

For a long time, his heart thumping, Jake looked waveringly back.

The wolf's unblinking stare was ravenous.

It had been searching for him, he thought, and it meant to have something from him. But before he could scream at it – either to go or come and take its dark gift the wolf pricked up its ears, turned and shambled away into the forest. Sick with relief Jake fled indoors.

"This will be the Game of Games," said Lizzy. "We'll call it – Children of the Stars."

She raised her arms then dramatically let them fall.

It was afternoon in the garage. Jake and Lizzy had cleared a magic circle amongst the belongings of both families.

Lizzy's uneven hair was tied in a cloth that had bits of mirror on it, giving her a prophetic star-strewn look. A velvet curtain was draped round her shoulders and when she moved, armloads of bangles clanked.

Jake's neck was prickling already. Shared magic was the best, the only kind he thought, for driving away the wolf. For the first time in months he was almost happy.

"But who are the Children of the Stars?" he asked.

When Lizzy made up a character for him it was as if she dipped her hand into the dark whirl of time and space, choosing a magic robe, a self to be, and at once, putting it on he felt taller, less afraid.

"Twin brother and sister of course," she said, "but not from this world."

"What world then?" he said.

Lizzy was silent for a long time before she said in the sing-song voice of the Game:

"The world from which all worlds come and all beginnings began. Everyone there has magic powers. It's the most beautiful place in the universe. But the terrible thing is—"

"Yes—" Jake held his breath.

"There was a wicked magician and he didn't want our parents to be happy. He let them think he was pleased they'd married but he was just biding his time. Then one day a terrible whirlwind came swirling down, splitting the darkness from the light and snatching us from our cradle."

"But how would we survi—" began Jake, but it was against the rules for him to interrupt. The magic was all Lizzy's. It was always through Lizzy the Game spoke. She swept on, glowering.

"And though we survived (with the help of a wise woman in the forest and her healing herbs)," she rattled off, "ever since then we've been wanderers from world to world, trying to get back to our own home."

Jake was dazzled. He was wrong to have doubted. This was Lizzy's best. With Lizzy he could do anything, be anyone.

"What's my name?" he said greedily. "What's my—"

The door between house and garage burst open. Jake's heart knocked against his ribs with rage.

"Don't mind me," said Max. "Carry on with your conspiracies, my dears. Just tell me who swiped my bloody pump."

"No one," said Lizzy, pointing. "It fell off. And we aren't conspiring. We're playing."

She stared back unflinching but she didn't tell Max to go, Jake thought. In fact, to his horror, she began chattering on again as if they were still alone.

"The problem is, the whirlwind was so violent that each of us lost part of ourselves and until we find it we can't use our true magic powers."

Having failed to impress, Max sauntered with maddening slowness to his pump, and even more slowly picked it up.

"That makes it impossible," said Jake. He didn't want to speak. But Lizzy was beaming around, delighted.

She likes an audience, he thought. The audience had always been Jake before.

"Not impossible," said Lizzy. "A challenge."

The door banged again. Jake let his breath go. It was all right. He should have realized Max would get bored if it wasn't mountain bikes or computers.

"Who are you *really* then?"

Lizzy dipped her fingers into the box of Woolworths jewellery left over from Children of the Island. Then tipping the treasure on to the dusty floor she plucked a pirate's plastic dagger from it, chanting:

"In the name of the Sun and the name of the Moon, I am Sephira, the sorceress—"

"You two are totally but totally bats," said Max,

sitting down heavily beside them, filling up the magic circle with his size eight basketball boots, and grinning his unpleasant grin. "Loopy. Deranged."

"I thought you'd gone," said Jake, white with shame and fury.

"It's only a game, isn't it? A pathetic little game. Then you'd better let me join in. We're all one jolly family now."

"Oh give him a chance, Jake," said Lizzy.

A chance!

If you gave Max Harris a chance he'd only use it to wreck anything someone else valued, the way he'd broken Jake's watch and chewed Lizzy's fake fur pencil case. Maybe Max hadn't started out obnoxious when he was small and gurgling in a white nightie. Neither had Attila the Hun and you wouldn't give either of them an inch. Maybe Max would have been a nicer boy if Ruth had got him earlier and hugged him till he turned back into a human being. Maybe Max was simply hungry for love. But that didn't mean you had to feed other people to him to keep him quiet, as if he was a shark in a tank.

"But who would he be – it was about us, Lizzy – it was—"

Jake couldn't put into words his vague awareness that through the magic of the Game Lizzy discovered wonderful truths. The Game had never been pretend to Jake. It was the truest thing he knew.

"But it isn't ever going to be just you two again, is it?" said Max, carefully levelling his hair with his palm. "Face facts, kiddo. The Owens are extinct. It's Harrises from now on, like it or not."

"*Not*," whispered Jake into his collar. Then all three jumped as the garage door went roaring up and over like a judgement. But it was only Ruth, holding a dirty plate at arm's length.

"Who put leftovers out into the garden? We'll get every stray for miles. And rats. Had you even thought about rats? It was you Jake, wasn't it? What were you trying to feed this time?"

"Just a dog," said Jake hoarsely. "It was very thin. I thought it might die. You could see it didn't belong to anyone."

He couldn't say he had stolen food for the wolf in the cowardly hope it would accept his substitute offering and return to its own winter world, closing that terrifying door behind it.

"All the same," said Ruth. Then she grinned. "Even St Francis wouldn't put out scraps in Hither Green," she said. "I'm sure there's a law."

Suddenly she registered the three children, squatting uneasily in the gloom. "All playing together, eh? Well, that's something."

She went off, leaving the garage door draughtily up.

"Well, who shall I be?" said Max, pretending to think. "I think I shall be Kyroth the Mighty. I'm seven feet tall, as green as a pickled cucumber and immensely powerful and I have an extra eye in the palm of my right hand that can see across galaxies—"

"You could be the brother we didn't know about," Lizzy interrupted excitedly. "And when we meet you we don't know who you are. We think you're our enemy."

Max wiped imaginary tears of laughter from his eyes. "Do you two always go on like this?"

"Not in front of strangers," said Jake bitterly. But he couldn't hide the truth from himself any longer. It was not just Max Harris from whom he had to protect himself now but Lizzy Harris, who for the sake of happy families would spill open secrets as easily as a box of junk treasure.

"Oh, Lizzy's all right," Jake heard Ruth say on the phone one night. "She's a survivor. It's Jake I worry about."

Ruth was right. Lizzy was a survivor. So was Max. Max because he took everything he could get his hands on, even things he didn't want or need. Lizzy because she gave everything away, even those things that were not hers to give.

It's Jake I worry about.

There were bright patches on his sister's cheeks.

"Max wants to know who you're going to be," she repeated, shrill.

He could lose his temper, rush out, refuse to have any more to do with them. One of Jake's moods. A moody child, ever since his father left.

Slow. Secretive. Difficult.

Jake had been hearing those words all his life, as though some hostile fairy had pronounced them at his christening. Lizzy was the good twin. The clever one. The one everyone loved. The one who believed in happy endings.

It's Jake I worry about.

Max wants to know who you're going to be.

Inside his chest was a hot and furious fist. It made him want to punch someone, anyone. There was a howling hole in his world and no one would fix it. Not his dad. Not Ruth. And now, he understood with every grieving cell of his body, not Lizzy. He would have to live around the charred and splintered edges of that hole forever and he couldn't bear the terror of it without Lizzy to tell him who to be.

Unless—

"Supposing I tell you who you are, Jakie boy," suggested Max. "I think you're a little—"

"No," said Jake quietly, surprising himself. "No thanks."

"Are you all right?" asked Lizzy. "You look weird."

Jake was staring out through the door into the street which as usual was bright and empty like a street in a science fiction film. The Owens' old street was bursting with life; quarrels, laughter, whistling. Perhaps one day the new street would be too. But for now they were in no-man's-land. Two families uneasily adrift with two sets of memories; lost wanderers every one.

"Jake?"

The street wasn't empty. It never had been. Under the cherry trees reality was thinning as though someone was breathing on a frosty plane to clear a space. But this space was a hole and it went on growing and the harsh winter wind came blowing out of it, burdened with cloudy presences, filling the street with a twilight layer of forest.

This time the coming of the wolf was a relief. Jake thought he must have called it somehow without knowing.

"Why's it so cold?" said Max uneasily.

A blizzard was billowing across the street in flying white shawls. Lizzy put up her hand and looked scared to find snowflakes in her hair.

He was wrong. The wolf hadn't come to take anything. It had come to remind him to take what belonged to him. It had come to remind Jake who he was. With snow blowing into his eyes and mouth he struggled for words.

"I'm Owen," he said at last. "And I'll always be Owen. Names mean something. Lizzy knows. That's why we take so long over it in the Game. It's like – your fate. You have to think before you change one."

Lizzy stared. For the first time in his life Jake had spoken with the voice of the Game and having begun, he didn't stop.

"When Sephira and I were stolen, my lost self went falling down and down, until it fluttered into the forest just as a new wolf cub was being born."

"Blimey, just like Tarzan," said Max, trying to grin. But his lips were blue. Jake couldn't tell if it was cold or fear. All he knew was the power of this new voice rushing through him like a wind.

"The wolves knew this cub was different but they brought it up just the same and taught it all a wolf needs to know. How to survive winter. How to find your way in the forest. But when the cub was grown they could see it was restless, that it needed to go out into the world and search for me. You see the wolf can never forget for one moment that he belongs to me but if I'm not careful I easily forget about him.

And then I lose my true powers. And so however far he travels through worlds and lifetimes, he's always joined to me by an invisible thread." He paused, only wanting to say what was true.

"And when I forget who I really am, the wolf—"

He raised his hand, pale, smiling, but never finished.

With the speed of an express train something hurtled at them, gathering itself to spring.

Max sprang back with a yelp, his face bleached with terror, blindly defending himself. Overhead, filling an immense space, Jake's wolf blotted out the afternoon like dirty snowcloud, all fangs and fury.

Then like a deadly hawk it plummeted.

"Don't, don't," Lizzy screamed. She covered her face but she couldn't shut out the shrieking whirlwind in her ears.

Then the wind died. Max moved first, backing away looking sick.

"I didn't see anything," he said through numb lips. "Not anything. And you'll never make me say I did." He bolted through the door into the house and went pounding upstairs.

Lizzy couldn't move even when Jake opened his eyes at last, brushing away melting crystals in a dazed way. She had to admit he didn't look any the worse for – whatever it was that had happened. In

fact he looked disgustingly well. More solid somehow. For the first time in his life her brother moved as if he trusted the earth under his feet.

"Did you see?" he asked.

There was no fear in his voice. Why wasn't he *afraid?*

"I don't know," said Lizzy still shuddering. "Not exactly. Well, it sort of went into you. Or you went into it. I couldn't look. It was horrible. I don't want to talk about it."

She tore off her Sephira clothes and ran into the house.

It didn't feel any lonelier after she had gone.

"In the name of the Sun and the name of the Moon," he whispered.

It wasn't Lizzy's fault she believed in the wrong sort of happy ending. It wasn't her fault she thought she had to give up being a magic Owen to make the Harrises happy. One day her missing self would find her, the way Jake's wolf had found him.

"I wish it had been something nicer," said Jake softly to himself, "not so hungry and desperate and bashed-up. But it was mine. It was my wolf."

Besides, Jake thought, both Jake and the wolf would change as they got to know each other. The wolf less savage and wintery. Jake no longer tame and scared.

Jacob Owen. A hero's name with enough room in it to allow for growing. He laughed to himself, picturing a huge roughly sewn jacket of wolfskin almost reaching to his ankles. He had a long way to go.

He could hear water running and Ruth banging pans, cooking supper in the little stopgap kitchen. He wouldn't go back into the house for a while. He'd give Max time to recover. He collected up Sephira's starry head-dress, her robe and knife and dropped them into the dressing-up box.

Lizzy had taught him the power of magic. It was up to him how he used it.

Getting down on the floor Jacob Owen began to pick up the scattered jewels, one by one.

The Green Ghost

Terry Tapp

Of one thing Emma Finch was absolutely certain: there is a life after death. She knew this as surely as she knew that night followed day, and she was quietly happy with her knowledge. Furthermore, Emma believed in ghosts. She believed in good ghosts and bad ghosts, and she most certainly believed in the Green Ghost that haunted Brampton Hall. What Emma did not know – and she intended to rectify that within the next few minutes – was whether Brampton Hall was *still* haunted by the Green Ghost of her childhood memories. After all, a lot can happen in eighty years.

Trudging up the steep, gravel drive to Brampton Hall, Emma was pleasantly surprised to note that the immense Victorian house had lost much of its bleak, forbidding appearance over the years. The bright blue curtains at each window were such a contrast to the deep brown curtains of her own era. And the garden was friendly too; a child's swing, a bicycle and a brightly coloured beach ball persuaded her that Brampton Hall was now a happy family home.

Now Emma stood before the massive oak door of Brampton Hall, her jaw set resolutely as she gripped the lion-head doorknocker and clamped it hard against the iron spike. Still holding the door-knocker, reluctant to let go of it, her mind spanned the years back to the time when people came to Brampton Hall on horseback, or in fine coaches. How many hands, she wondered, have gripped this very doorknocker?

Emma was about to knock again when she noticed a new bell-push set into the door jamb; she pressed it once. The resulting pandemonium caused her to jump back from the door in alarm. Two gigantic, hairy, barking, bounding, rollicking, shapeless dogs skidded joyfully around the house to greet her.

"Oh!" Emma cried. "Down, boys. You'll get my coat dirty."

She pressed the bell again, twice this time, her eyes fixed on the dogs as they barked and scampered around her, darting in at her legs, then turning away at the very last moment.

With some relief she heard the door bolt slide back and she smiled at the little girl who stood there, thumb in mouth, a scowl upon her pretty young face.

"Hello," said Emma. "Is your daddy or mummy at home?"

The child stared vacantly at her.

"Well?" Emma gave the girl an encouraging smile. "Are they?"

The child considered the question awhile, appearing to make some decision, and slammed the door hard in Emma's face, causing the two dogs, who had been watching events with pricked ears, to jump to their feet and set up a terrible row. After what seemed like a lifetime all over again, the door opened and the girl reappeared, thumb still wedged in her mouth.

"Yes," she said. "Mummy is here."

"I wonder if I might have a word with her."

Thumbsucker considered that question, too, as if everything Emma said demanded the utmost thought. Suddenly, without warning, she removed her thumb from her mouth and shouted at the top of her voice: "Mummy! There's an old lady here and she wants to talk to you!"

"An old lady?" That was a boy's voice.

"What – a witch?" A younger boy shouted that.

"No," said Thumbsucker. "She isn't a witch. She's just very, very old."

By now the two boys had clattered down the stairs and were standing before Emma, inspecting her with the unashamed curiosity children sometimes display.

"What does she want?" asked the smaller boy.

"Dunno," said Thumbsucker.

Then the dogs started barking again, bored with listening to human conversation. The two boys let out ear-piercing whoops and shot from the doorway like arrows, chasing the delighted dogs back around the house where they had come from.

As Emma turned back to face Thumbsucker, she saw a young woman hurrying towards the door, wiping her hands on her apron.

"What is it?" she asked.

"This old woman," said Thumbsucker. "She wants you for something."

"Really!" The child's mother made an exasperated face. Then smiled at Emma. "Sorry to have kept you waiting – I didn't know if there was really someone at the door, or if she was playing a trick."

"Lovely children," Emma said.

"Lovely, *rude* children," was the reply. "I do apologize for their bad manners."

"Please, don't apologize," said Emma. "They are right, you know – I *am* an old lady. Sometimes I have to be reminded of the fact."

They both laughed at that, and then Emma explained the reason for her visit. "I would, very much, like to look over Brampton Hall again."

"Again?"

"Yes, I used to live here."

"Oh, really?"

"My entire childhood was spent in this very house, and it would be nice to view it."

The young woman looked puzzled. "View? Brampton Hall is not for sale, you know."

"I realize that," Emma said. "Anyway, I couldn't afford it even if it *was* for sale. What would I do with a large place like this to keep up?"

"Well, perhaps you had better come inside," said the woman. "My name is Jean Williams, by the way."

"I'm Miss Finch," Emma said. "Miss Emma Finch."

She stepped into the hallway and stared around her. The place had hardly changed at all over the years; it was uncanny. She breathed in the rich, lingering woody smell as she surveyed the carved wall panels. Suddenly, she was a child again, as she relived the memories so vividly. She could hear the laughter and the household noises of her childhood as plainly as if they were happening that very moment. Games of tag along the corridors, the sweet enticing aroma of spiced cooking. It was all returning, unharmed by the voyage of years. Now she could see the rosy-faced cook, wide-eyed and smiling with pride as she carried the platter of Christmas meats, the pert faces of the two young housemaids watching the proceedings, yet struggling to keep hidden. Emma had adored the maids.

Now there was the smell of apples and woodsmoke, evoking autumn and shortening days. When Emma looked at the parlour door, she could almost hear the low, grumbling conversation of her father. What a serious man he was.

"Miss Finch?"

Emma looked at the young woman in mild surprise.

"You may have a look around if you wish," said Mrs Williams with a smile. "I've been talking to you – but you were miles away."

"Was I?" Then Emma realized that she had been so absorbed in her memories, she had lost track of the present. "Yes, I suppose I was. It really is quite an exhilarating experience returning to Brampton Hall. I had such a happy childhood here."

Mrs Williams smiled. "Is this the first time you have seen Brampton Hall since your childhood?"

"The first time I have been inside," said Emma. "I have, on many occasions, passed by and glanced up the driveway, not daring to knock at the door."

"Well, you feel free to walk around as you please. You must forgive the children's bedrooms. I have told them that they must keep their own rooms tidy and, I'm afraid, they aren't very good at it yet. I'm determined to let the rooms go until they learn their lesson."

"I'm sorry if I have called at an inconvenient time," Emma said.

"It's no trouble."

"You are very kind."

"If you will excuse me, then . . ." said Mrs Williams, making for the stairs. "I really do have a lot of work to get through." Emma nodded absently, already absorbed in memories.

"I'll be in the kitchen," Mrs Williams told her. "And if the children start to make nuisances of themselves, send them to me."

"I will," Emma promised. "Thank you."

Standing on the bottom tread of the wide, twisting staircase, Emma looked up at the stained-glass windows, recalling how, on a bright summer day, the sun would tumble through the coloured glass and light up the whole hall like a carnival. She smiled, happy that the memories had not faded with the years; in fact, if anything, the memories had been enhanced by the passing of time. Once again she placed her gloved hand on the polished balustrade and then, on impulse, removed the glove so that she could feel the hard, enduring wood.

Slowly, savouring every step like a fine meal, Emma walked up the staircase, memories flooding in on her so fast that she had, at times, to stop and wait until the kaleidoscope of faces and events had settled in her mind. Each step disturbed the dusts of forgetfulness, and she was amazed at the things which she was able to remember, amazed and delighted.

There had been no major structural changes in the old house, and Emma was able to locate the rooms confidently. She turned at the top of the stairs, walked along to the far end of the narrow corridor which led to the servants' annexe and decided to explore the east wing first. The door of the master bedroom was ajar. Emma tapped gently, waited for a reply and, when there was none, she stepped into the room, her heart pounding against her ribs.

Full circle, Emma thought. Return to the birthplace.

The room was bathed in mellow, yellow sunlight which splashed the walls and furniture like butter. It was, Emma considered, miraculous how little the room had changed in appearance. The Italian marble fireplace still looked new, and the ornate ceiling was as perfect now as it was in her memory. Apart from the addition of some rather bright wallpaper and several pictures, the room was timeless and unchanged.

"What are you looking for?"

Emma wheeled around, startled at the unexpected intrusion of the child's voice. Thumbsucker was standing in the doorway, her thumb still lodged in her mouth.

"I'm not looking *for* anything," said Emma. "I'm looking *at* things."

"What are you looking at?"

"Everything," Emma replied. "I just want to look at everything and remember how the house used to be. You know, apart from the fact that we had oil lighting, then gaslight, the house is much the same as when I was your age."

"Gaslight?"

"Yes," said Emma. "We used to have a centre light in this room and wall brackets over there." She indicated the far wall.

"Do you want to see my room?" Thumbsucker asked.

Emma smiled at her; she was a pretty child, about seven years old with small, rather pert features.

"I would love to see your room," she said. "Lead the way."

The little girl removed her thumb from her mouth and offered her hand to Emma, who pretended not to notice; she certainly did not want to hold that sticky, wet little hand. From the master bedroom, they went out to the corridor, along the landing above the stairs until they reached the four smaller bedrooms. "This is mine," said Thumbsucker, kicking the door open with her foot.

"How lovely!" Emma cried, thinking exactly the opposite. The room was a jumble of toys, books, dolls and clothes. "My, this is a bright little room." She had to tread most carefully in order to avoid treading on the toys which were strewn across the floor.

"I fink it's awful," Thumbsucker said. "Mummy says she won't tidy it up for me."

"Quite right, too."

"But it's in such a mess."

"And who made it into such a mess?" Emma asked, trying to keep a straight face.

"It jus' happened," Thumbsucker replied. "Do you like my wallpaper?"

Following the young girl's gaze, Emma surveyed the psychedelic paper which covered the chimney breast. It was a brightly coloured paper, screaming, sickening, gaudy and busy-looking. "It is very — unusual," Emma said, feeling almost giddy as she groped for the edge of the bed. "Yes, very unusual indeed."

"Robin chose it for himself," Thumbsucker said. "He got Daddy to buy the paper."

"Did Robin used to sleep here?"

"Only for a while," said Thumbsucker. "Then he got scared, and I had to sleep here."

"Scared?"

Thumbsucker nodded vigorously.

"What was he scared of?"

"Ghosts," the child replied. "Robin is scared of ghosts."

"And he thought there were ghosts in this room?"

"There *was* a ghost here," Thumbsucker said. "Robin saw it and he cried."

"Have you seen it?" Emma asked, trying to keep her voice as calm as possible.

"I saw it – once."

"Were you frightened?" Now Emma was excited. Was it possible that Thumbsucker had seen the ghost of her childhood? It was very important to Emma to know the answer. But the child was engrossed in rummaging through her toys, apparently having lost all interest in the conversation. Determined to get an answer, Emma reached down and lifted the child on to her lap.

"You went a funny colour when you lifted me," Thumbsucker observed seriously.

"I expect I did," Emma said. "Sometimes I forget myself and do things which I ought not to do."

"So do I," Thumbsucker said confidently. "Yesterday I made a cake in the kitchen and Mummy told me off for making a mess."

"How long ago did you see the ghost?" Emma asked.

"Last year."

"I would be most interested to hear all about it," Emma said, trying very hard to conceal her impatience. "Would you like to tell me the story, starting from the very beginning?"

Thumbsucker gazed up at the ceiling as if searching for inspiration, her face creased in concentration. Sucking hard on her thumb, the girl started to speak. Emma gently took her wrist and pulled the thumb from the girl's mouth so she could hear what she was saying.

"You got bony knees," Thumbsucker told her, with the candid truthfulness of the very young.

"Yes, I know," Emma said. "But you must tell me about the ghost. It is very important to me."

"Well, it all started when Robin asked Daddy for this wallpaper," Thumbsucker said. Emma listened as the child related the tale, interrupting now and then to make quite sure that she had heard correctly, for Thumbsucker kept pushing her thumb back into her mouth out of habit.

It seemed that Robin had set his heart on the bedroom as soon as they had moved in, because he wanted to make it into his private den. Against his own better judgement, Mr Williams had promised Robin that he might choose his own decorations, and the result of that had been the psychedelic wallpaper. But, within a few days of moving into the room, Robin had started to complain of funny noises and voices which kept him awake at nights.

"The room is haunted," Robin had told his father.

Mr Williams would not hear of such a thing. "Nonsense," he had told Robin sternly. "There are no such things as ghosts."

Thumbsucker had, of course, been enchanted by tales of hauntings and she had begged Robin to exchange rooms with her.

"But didn't the thought of seeing a ghost frighten you?" Emma asked.

"I *wanted* to see him," said Thumbsucker.

"So you exchanged rooms with Robin. What happened next?"

Thumbsucker began to tell the story of her first night in the room, and Emma listened eagerly, remembering the nights that she had spent in that very room. It was uncanny how very similar the stories were.

"After I had kissed Mummy goodnight, I tried to go to sleep right away," said Thumbsucker, her face rumpled with deep frowns as she concentrated. "It was hard getting to sleep in a new room, and I kept waking up because there were funny noises going on. I had to sleep in Robin's old bed and it's got all lumps in it and his pillow is harder than mine. I stayed awake for hours. I even heard Daddy and Mummy come up to bed."

"My!" said Emma. "That must have been very late indeed."

"It was," said Thumbsucker. "Anyway, that's when the green smoke came."

"Green smoke?" Emma asked, her voice trembling

with excitement.

"Yes, green smoke. I was looking over at Bunnylite when I suddenly saw green smoke drifting up from my bed."

"Good gracious!" Emma said. "What did you do?"

"I was frightened at first. I thought my bed was on fire. Then the smoke sort of hung in the air and I could see a green light in the very centre of it."

"Luminous," said Emma.

"The green light got brighter and brighter, lighting up the room until it was brighter than Bunnylite. Through the mistiness, I thought I could see a face. Then, after a while, the face became clearer and I could see that it was an old, old man. He was even older than you."

"Then he must have been very ancient," Emma said without a trace of a smile.

"The old man had a green face and it was covered with warts," Thumbsucker said, her eyes wide open as she recalled the horrible apparition. "He was screaming at me, his eyes alight like fire."

"The Green Ghost of Brampton Hall," Emma whispered, but Thumbsucker was too immersed in her story to hear.

"It was cold, even in my bed, and I could see that the ghost was coming for me. I wanted to hide my head under the bedclothes, but I was too scared. He

laughed, showing all his bad teeth, and when his mouth was opened wide I could see that, instead of a tongue, he had a snake!"

"A snake?" cried Emma, holding Thumbsucker close for comfort as if she were a doll. How many times had she seen that precise nightmarish face?

"It was a snake, coiling in the ghost's mouth, hissing at me. The ghost came nearer until his face was almost touching mine and then he opened his mouth again and the snake slid out, over his chin, and dangled in front of my face. I cried."

"I know," said Emma, rocking the child. "I know. It is a truly dreadful thing to see."

"Then he started to grow bigger, laughing all the

time. It was as if he had taken a deep breath and his whole body swelled up. He filled up the room with his body and his laughing. His hands were near my face, and his fingers were long and knobbly, with nails like claws. The nails were bright red."

But Emma wasn't even listening now; she had become absorbed in her own memories of the evil ghost. She, too, felt the chill and the dank, cold clamminess as she recalled those terrible nights when the Green Ghost had haunted Brampton Hall.

"Then his talons touched my face," Emma said, completely oblivious of the fact that she had interrupted Thumbsucker. "His talons bore down on me, burning and scratching. And his eyes! They were bright, like emeralds, and so very, very evil." Emma was living her childhood again. She could see the malevolent, fluorescent face as it leered at her; she could feel those burning claws and smell the cold, dank smell of decaying food. "So he is still here," she said, realizing that she was frightening Thumbsucker.

"No."

"What do you mean?"

"He frightened me, so I sent him packing."

"How did you manage to do that?"

"Well, I thought it was very clever the way he kept changing shape, but I didn't like the funder."

"Funder?"

"Yes, it was loud funder and there wasn't any lightning."

"Ah – thunder," Emma said.

"It was very loud – much louder than his laughing. The noise was making my room shake, and I got scared in case Daddy thought it was me making all the noise. I get blamed for everything around here."

Emma smiled. "Do you, indeed?"

"That's when I told him to buzz off."

"You told the Green Ghost of Brampton Hall to buzz off?"

"Yes," said Thumbsucker. "I told him that he was making too much noise. So he went."

"What? You mean he just disappeared?"

"He sort of melted," said Thumbsucker thoughtfully. "It was like butter on toast. His green face seemed to melt and the smoke became thinner until he was all gone."

"How very brave of you," Emma said.

"I still don't understand why he just went when I told him to."

"You probably shamed him into it," said Emma. "Hurt his professional pride, no doubt. Nothing could be more demoralizing for a ghost than to be told to buzz off. Now, think very, very carefully. Have you ever seen him since?"

"No. He hasn't been back."

"How about other ghosts?"

"Other ghosts?"

"Yes. Have you ever seen a different ghost to the Green Ghost of Brampton Hall?"

"No," Thumbsucker said. "Do you think there will be one?"

"I shouldn't be surprised at all," Emma said. "Usually a house is visited by just one ghost, but if he disappears another ghost may sometimes take his place."

"I haven't seen one," Thumbsucker said.

"You are sure?"

"Yes. I would know if I had."

"Of course you would," said Emma. "Of course."

She got up from the bed, a smile upon her face, her eyes alight with happiness. "So the Green Ghost has gone at last."

"Come on," said Thumbsucker. "I'll show you the rest of the house. Would you like to see Robin's room?"

"Yes, that would be nice."

"After that we can see Philip's room, and then I can show you Daddy's study."

Emma followed the child, drinking in the memories as she entered each room. Everything — everything that mattered — was substantially the same. The house was still alive with people, and the bricks and slates were still there. The floors were the same floors which she, as a child, had scampered across. Even the fifth stair from the top still creaked loudly when it was trodden on. Somehow Emma had the feeling that Brampton Hall was indestructible; built before she was born, it would still be there, strong and immovable, long after she was dead and forgotten. It was a monument, in brick and stone, to Emma's happy childhood. Yes, Brampton Hall would endure to see many generations come and go.

It was a satisfying thought.

"I hope she isn't bothering you," said Mrs Williams, appearing suddenly at the foot of the stairs. "I could hear her chattering away all the time."

"On the contrary," said Emma. "We have had a most interesting discussion."

"And I haven't been naughty," Thumbsucker added.

Emma started down the stairs, smiling as her foot touched the fifth one from the top. "You have been most kind to allow me this visit. I have enjoyed it so much."

"You are welcome," Mrs Williams replied. "Now you must come into the kitchen and have a cup of tea. I've just made a fresh pot."

So they went into the big, warm kitchen, and Emma was delighted to see that the old kitchen range was still in use, sparkling as brightly as ever it did when she was young. The thick, crackling logs burned red and cosy, sending busy flames up to the massive iron kettle which sang and sighed in ecstasy. The whole house breathed contentment.

"Well?" asked Mrs Williams. "Do you still like your old home?"

"I love it," Emma said fervently. "It will do very nicely indeed, I am sure of that."

"Do?" asked Mrs Williams.

"Oh, yes. Very nicely indeed," Emma replied absently. "Especially now that the Green Ghost is gone."

"Green Ghost? Ah, you've been listening to make-believe stories," said Mrs Williams as she poured out a cup of tea and offered Emma a plate of home-made cakes.

They talked for nearly an hour, Emma delighting Mrs Williams with her reminiscences. When it was time for Emma to leave, she insisted on giving Thumbsucker fifty pence for telling her about the Green Ghost. "I am so glad he has gone," she said.

"Please come again," Mrs Williams said as she saw Emma to the door. "I enjoyed hearing about Brampton Hall as it was all those years ago."

"I will," Emma promised. "I'd love to come again."

But Emma never did return to Brampton Hall to delight Mrs Williams with more stories of her childhood. She waved goodbye and trudged back down the crunchy gravel drive, her heart beating excitedly. She smiled, turned and waved and was gone.

Some months later, as Thumbsucker lay upon her bed, in the throes of sticking Christmas cards into her scrapbook, Emma came to her and sat on the edge of the bed.

"Where did you come from?" asked Thumbsucker.

"I just came," Emma said happily.

"Do you want to see around the house again?"

"No, thank you," Emma replied. "I've come to stay, this time. I'm going to stay here for ever and ever."

"Until you die?" asked Thumbsucker.

"Until I get told to buzz off," Emma replied with a twinkle in her eye.

"I wouldn't ever tell you to buzz off," Thumbsucker said. "I like having you here."

"That is nice to hear," Emma replied. "I'll try very hard not to make a nuisance of myself." Then she rose from the bed, crossed the room and floated straight through the bedroom door.

Somebody Lives in the Nobody House

Ruth Park

Some people can tell you a ghost story that happened to their great-grandfather, or their neighbour's aunt in Moonee Ponds. But my spooky story happened to me, Sally Gavin, and only last year. On the day after my eleventh birthday, as a matter of fact.

I still often think of that late afternoon – the Ferryman's Arms beside the weedy river, its windows red with a sunset that wasn't really happening. And then, later on, when Fenella and I were alone in that dim cobwebby room, and time had become tangled up somehow, and we heard that croaky old man's voice coming from nowhere. The memory still makes me shiver, and Fenella feels the same way.

My sister Fenella was nine at the time of the ghost.

Mum must have been round the twist when she gave her that romantic name, for Fenella at nine was as romantic as a mixmaster. A bossy, know-all kid, with a tongue hung in the middle. Around home she was known as The Blob, or Orrible, or Dr No. She's different now, a cheerful tearaway, and we all like her much more.

Dad and Fenella and I were driving along this clay horror stretch in the Northern Rivers country. Mum had intended to come, but our brother Robbie had burst out with chickenpox, and so she was home with him, no doubt very pleased to be spared the inevitable hardships of Dad's expeditions.

Dad is a pernickety driver, and when he saw a police cycle coming up fast on his right, he looked offended. He pulled over, and this Martian did a wheelie through the puddles and showered the car with dirt. He took off his helmet and stuck his face into the window, grinning. Rather nice. He said he was Constable Fiddler from Burangie, the tiny township we'd zizzed through some five kilometres or so back.

"Dan Gavin," said Dad civilly.

"Dad was NOT speeding," said Fenella in her loud, set-down voice. "I was personally keeping an eye on the dial."

The young constable laughed. "It's just that Des

Harris at the service station told me you'd mentioned you were going through to the old Ferryman pub tonight."

"Dad may buy it and turn it into a motel," announced Orrible. Dad gave her one of his belt-up looks and explained to the officer that he was just going to look the place over. He had never as much as seen a good photograph of it.

The constable pensively scratched the red welt the helmet had left on his forehead. "I was just thinking," he said. "Maybe you don't know the place is derelict, nothing but rats and dry rot. It hasn't been occupied for forty years or more. People around here called it the Nobody House."

"I suppose they say it's haunted!" said Fenella scornfully.

Dad explained that we didn't intend actually dossing in the old building. Our car has a camping body, and anyway, Dad had this junior-school love for sleeping under a tree in his old sleeping-bag. You could see he wasn't going to be done out of that.

He listened impatiently to the young constable, as he said, "Just the same, Mr Gavin, I wish you'd reconsider. It's getting dark quickly, the road's a shocker, the bridge at the ferry's nothing to write home about, and after all the rain we've had lately there'll be mud in all directions. Why not drive back and spend the night at Burangie pub and come out this way again tomorrow?"

Of course Constable Fiddler knew that area better than we did, and what he said made sense. But instantly Fenella put on a demo. She had not only been promised she could camp in the car, she was also chief cook for the trip and had brought sausages and tomatoes to fry on the portable stove, and Dad was not being just, and justice was needed in the world of today, because just look at Rhodesia, and aboriginal land rights and Zoos. Well, actually, just before she got to Zoos Dad became bored with the whole thing and said he'd drive on a few kilometres and if the weather turned worse, he'd return to Burangie.

"Your decision. OK?" said Constable Fiddler, a bit sharply, I thought, and he turned once more into a Martian and did another wheelie that spattered our car from head to tail. Dad drove on in a temper.

The countryside looked soaked to the skin. In the foothills ahead of us silky-oaks were blooming, custard yellow against the storm clouds. You could see rainshowers tearing themselves away, spinning into willywillies of drops and then petering out in mid-air. The road was less rutted now, but it had a slick, yukky surface and Dad drove very carefully. All at once I noticed someone standing beside the road, waving. In that sodden, lonely landscape another human being was the last thing I had expected to see. Dad stopped.

"Need a lift, mate? We're only going as far as the old Ferryman, though."

"That'll do grand. Much obliged, mister."

It was a boy three or four years older than myself, dressed in worn overalls. He had a grain sack over his shoulders as though he expected a downpour any minute. As he slid into the back seat he half-smiled at me. He had one of those shy clean country faces and crooked teeth.

Naturally Fenella turned around at once and treated our passenger to a recountal of how we lived in the Blue Mountains outside Sydney; her teacher believed she was going to amount to something with the violin (she hasn't yet); Dad specialized in ferreting out old properties and doing them up for a motel chain; Robbie had the chickenpox, and she was going to fry the sausages as soon as we camped because she was ravishing. She meant ravenous, of course, and I saw a grin flit over the boy's face.

"Lonesome out there," said the boy. "Better to spend the night in town, I reckon."

"Why?" asked Fenella. The boy didn't answer so Dad asked if the bridge were dangerous.

"I guess she's all right," said the boy. "Used to be

dangerous when the river ran a banker, got carried away once and someone got drowned. No, I was just thinking, there's heavy weather on the way and you might get bogged and that."

"We'll chance it," said Dad. I could see he was testy because of all the discouragement he was getting. Before Orrible could launch into her speech about how sport was for dummos and she was learning chess, I asked the boy where he lived.

"Not far," he said. I was going to ask how he got into Burangie to school, when we came to the top of the hill, and there before us was the river, and willows and casuarinas, and amongst them the most picturesque old inn, like something out of a Victorian book. It was a Georgian building, with tiny-paned windows, and a rounded veranda curving about the house to shelter the lower storey. There were half a dozen chimneys of yellow brick, topped with twisty chimney pots, and to one side a stableyard with a high arched gateway of stone. Of course I knew that the Ferryman's Arms had once been a staging-post for Cobb and Co coaches, and I imagined them sweeping down this very hill, jingling and creaking, the coachman blowing his horn, the passengers looking forward to a supper of roast mutton and boiled currant pudding in the parlour and then a night's sleep between clean sheets.

"I suppose they drove right on to a big ferry punt?" asked Dad.

"That's so, mister," replied the boy, pointing. "Down there by the she-oaks and where the bridge is now. The ferrymen pulled the punt over with ropes and weights. But the river's nearly all silted up now. It only runs at times like that, after weeks of heavy rain."

"Just look at the way the sunset is reflected in those old windows," I said. "You'd swear people lived there. That's not a Nobody House."

I couldn't take my eyes off the place. It looked so homely, so cosy in the shelter of the big dark hills. We drove down the grade and Dad crept over the bridge in second gear. But it seemed solid enough.

It was true what the boy had said – the river was almost swamp. The bed had been taken over by reeds and coarse grass, and the water was muddy, with crusts of yellow bubbles. When we drove into the stableyard, it was full of mouldy rubbish – broken casks and iron wheelrims and rotten timber. Moss grew between the paving stones, and there was a pump with an iron handle red with rust. Beyond were stables, their half-doors hanging, their interiors dark and forbidding.

But Dad didn't seem to find it disagreeable. "I think we'll camp right here," he said. "What do you say, Sally? There's a bit of overhang from the veranda if the rain comes down again."

As he spoke there was a long roll of thunder as though someone had run a stick around a huge bell. The boy shivered. Fenella spiked him with her inquisitive glance.

"You're scared! Do you think it's haunted?"

The boy looked away in his shy way. "There's talk of a ghost, all right."

He was going to say something else but off went Fenella, in her best Orrible manner, hammering that poor boy into the ground with scoffings. He looked embarrassed. Dad and I stood there looking at the inn, and I knew he was thinking the same thing as I was, how welcoming it was, with its broken windows shining crimson in the sunset. Then all at once I realized something. The sun had set half an hour or more before.

"Well then," said Fenella, who was now beside us, "the lights have been put on. The poor old ghost who lives in the Nobody House is afraid of the dark!"

But the power poles had finished on the other side of the river; I had noticed particularly. And though the daylight hadn't quite gone, and frogs were blurting down in the reeds and mosquitoes were whining around, I began to feel a bit queer.

Dad and I think alike. He said, as though to

himself, "Of course there are such things as generators." Then he said loudly and cheerfully, "Must be someone here after all. I'll just go and see. Start unpacking the grub, kids. I won't be long."

I had this impulse to say, "No, Dad, don't!" But he leaped on the veranda and marched along to the big front door, which stood wide open, half off its hinges. Its pretty shell-shaped fanlight was shattered to bits. I heard Dad call, "Hello in there, anyone at home?"

Just then all the lights went out. In the moment before my eyes became used to the twilight, I saw the lightning blinking in the mountains of cloud above. Fenella said severely, "What a dumb thing for Dad to do! The floor might be all rotten and he didn't even take the torch."

The torch was in the glove-box, so I struck my head inside the car and said, "Hand me the torch, will you. You'll find it inside the . . ."

But the car was empty. I got the torch myself and shone it around the stableyard but there was no sign of the boy. He must have slipped out of the car and gone off to wherever he lived. I felt a bit disgusted that he hadn't even said thanks to Dad for the lift, but I supposed he was keen to get back to the pigfarm or whatever it was before the storm broke. Orrible, however, thought he'd got peeved because she rubbished him about ghosts.

"He looked pretty sore," she said triumphantly.

"Oh, shut up," I said, "and let's go and find Dad. He must be bashing around inside there in the dark."

The front-door steps were overgrown with fennel and half-dead hydrangeas, and slimy with wet and decay. I called, "Dad, we've got the torch," and shone it round inside the door. The interior was just like a cave, huge and dark and full of rubbish. Something twinkled, and both Fenella and I jumped, but it was only a sliver of broken mirror with golden writing on it, behind an immense half-wrecked timber counter.

"This must have been the bar," I said.

Fenella shouted rudely, "OK, parent, no jokes, where are you?"

Then I saw a line of footprints in the dust which lay on the floor like grey down. They led to a half-open door beside the bar. I knew Dad wasn't one to play jokes – not on us, anyway – and I couldn't imagine why he would have gone straight into that little room. I imagined him fallen down a hole in the floor boards, fractured skull, and goodness knows what else. So I was annoyed when I felt Fenella pressing uneasily against me.

"I don't like all those mirrors, Sally," she whispered, and indeed the effect of those unexpected flashes, dim and cobwebby as they were, as I turned the torch this way and that, was so scary that I growled, "Stop telling me what you don't like!"

We went over to the half-open door and pushed and it opened with the regulation TV haunted house creak. Fenella giggled half-wittedly. I called, "You in here, Dad? Dad?"

He wasn't. It was a sort of little office, with a tottery desk piled with dirty old account books and an old-fashioned black telephone on the wall. Vandals had been in, I suppose: there were torn papers and footmarks all over the floor. Fenella said in a voice that was actually shaky, "Maybe he went upstairs."

I thought that unlikely in the dim light and all, but I felt so jumpy that I gladly agreed, "That's it. We'll go back into the bar and look for the stairs."

Right then, sudden as a gunshot, a voice said, "Go away! Go away! No peace anywhere!"

They talk about being paralysed with shock. Well, Fenella and I really were. Then Fenella gave a quavering snort.

"Sssssh!" I whispered. I knew the voice wasn't Dad's, or the boy's, either.

"I can't help it," gasped Orrible. She grabbed me with a grip like a wrestler's.

All I could think of was getting out of there. And all the time this croaky old voice was sort of breathing, somewhere beyond the office door, "A man can't find peace anywhere. That's all I want, peace . . ."

The lightning went off like a photoflash, and both of us saw someone was standing in the doorway. It was the figure of an old, old man, the queerest, raggiest old man I ever saw. He had a beard and a tattered hat that kept the rest of his face in shadow. I was petrified. I couldn't even point the torch at him. Fenella bored her head into my neck. She was shaking like a leaf. Then the old man kind of faded back into the shadows, and we heard that complaining voice getting fainter.

"Why don't they go away and leave me in peace?"

We clung to each other like two monkeys. My sister was sobbing out loud now. "It must be the ghost that haunts the hotel. And it's done something awful to Daddy."

I think my blood stopped circulating then, for now I heard footsteps out in the empty bar room. Fenella gave a terrifying squawk, and then Dad's voice called, "That you, Sally? Where the heck ARE you kids?"

The next moment he was in the office, as mad as a hornet. "Why the devil didn't you stay by the car, you young twits?"

"We came in to look for you, of course," hiccupped Fenella, "after the lights went out."

"But that was only a moment ago," protested Dad.

"It certainly was not," I said, angry now. "It must have been twenty minutes. We've been walking around, searching and calling. We thought maybe you'd fallen through the floor."

"Queer," murmured Dad. "Now that I come to think of it, everything seemed extraordinarily silent, almost uncanny. Then I heard young Orrible snort or something."

Fenella began to cry again, while I told Dad what we'd seen and heard. He didn't rubbish me.

Fenella blurted, "That boy we picked up, HE ran away. He was scared because he knew all the while that this nasty place is haunted."

Dad gave us both a hug. "Whatever it was you saw, I've had enough of it. We'll clear out for Burangie right away. The rain's started and I'm blowed if I'm going to spend a miserable wet night with two kids both babbling about spooks."

The phone rang. Fenella jumped and shrieked. Dad said tetchily, "Oh, turn it up, Blob. It's probably only that Constable Thing ringing to say the river's rising or something."

He took the receiver off its hook. "Hello, hello? Dan Gavin here. Who's that? Hello? Can you hear me?"

I had stopped being terrified. I was just awed. I kept saying, "Dad. Dad."

He shushed me. "Damn these country exchanges, can't make out more than a word here and there. Oh, shut UP, Sal! WHAT? Speak louder, man!"

"Dad," I said. "The phone isn't connected. Look at the wires, Dad, not connected for years."

"Ah, what's the use," he said. He put the phone back on the hook. "All I could make out was something about the river coming up, and some babble about the bridge. Sally, what's the matter? You're as white as paper."

I showed him the corroded ends of the wires.

Well, he took the torch and had us out of that place and into the car in four seconds flat. The rain was pelting down. The engine wouldn't start. Dad said, "Oh, dear heavens, not now." He pulled out the choke and she fired. We backed out of the stableyard, and the headlamps cast a yellow fan over the debris. It looked so sad and lonely, the way the old ghost had sounded.

Fenella had her head out the window, directing Dad as he turned to get on to the bridge. She squealed, "There he is, the ghost, standing in the doorway!"

The lights showed him up like a figure in a faded old photo. Dad put the car in gear with the kind of grind he'd murder poor Mum for, and we clattered over the bridge. All the reedy part was now under water, and the lowest boughs of the trees were awash. I knew any moment now the river would be over the bridge decking. I kept thinking about the disconnected phone, someone had warned us, but who, and why? Then Fenella, who was kneeling on the rear seat looking through the back window, croaked, "Dad, he's following us across the bridge. The ghost, Daddy!"

Dad jammed on the brakes. I shouted, "Don't stop! He might catch us up, he's halfway across the bridge already."

"Be quiet, Sally," said Dad curtly. "I've had enough of this. I'm ashamed of myself."

He opened the door and the rain stabbed in.

"He'll get you!" shrieked Fenella. Dad slammed the door. By the dim light of the rearlights and the occasional flash of lightning we saw him run towards the ghost, who was staggering and splashing through water already knee-high. We saw Dad grab the figure.

"It's not a ghost at all, it's just a poor fallen-down old man," shouted Fenella and in a flash she was out of the car and splashing through the rain to help Dad drag the man along. So I was the one who saw what happened.

First of all there was a long deep low roar, away off, in the hills, it seemed. And all the lights in the Ferryman's Arms went on. Every window shone; light poured out the open door and lit up the stableyard, the trees. It was beautiful, the very picture of an old inn waiting to welcome weary travellers. Then I saw the shape of the hill behind it changing. For a moment I couldn't believe it, then my sense came back to me and I, too, leaped out of the car and raced to help Dad and Fenella.

"It's a landslide," I shouted. "The whole hill's coming down on the Ferryman!"

The roar was fearsome, like surf.

Somehow we pushed and pulled the old man into the back seat. Dad drove like fury maybe six or seven hundred metres from the river. Then we stopped and just looked, mesmerized, as that hill came down on the building. It was no use speaking; nothing could be heard over the grinding, grating thunder of the avalanche. The old inn crumpled up, slid towards the flooding river with all its lights blazing. It was pushed like a toy in front of a torrent of mud. Then the lights went out, and we couldn't see anything. The roar had stopped, they were only rushing glugging sounds.

It was a terrible drive back to Burangie. The old man seemed almost unconscious. It was a relief when we saw headlights coming towards us. Not only Constable Fiddler in a car, but two other vehicles with several men in each, including the police sergeant.

"We should have listened to you, Constable," said Dad. He looked knocked-out, and like the rest of us he was as wet as a sponge. The sergeant said that the river was running a banker at Burangie too, and he'd thought perhaps the bridge would go and we'd be marooned. Dad was about to explain what had happened when the old man on the back seat stirred and said feebly, "Saved me life they did, saved me life."

The men gathered around, "It's Pop Trivett, what d'you know? Where'd you spring from, Pop?"

"Saved me life," whispered the old man. "I come down from me claim when the big wet started and holed up in the old ruin, snug as a bug. Woke up and heard folk talking and thought they was ghosts."

"Silly," said Fenella. "It was us."

"I was pretty riled," said the old man. "Ghosts mooning around, waking a man up. A man needs his peace and quiet. Then when I heard the car start I knew I'd made a bloomer. Lucky I got woke up though, because then I heard the landslide beginning up in the hills and I went for me life. But I couldn'ta made it without the gent and the girls here."

You're thinking that I've tricked you, that this isn't a ghost story but a we-thought-it-was-a-ghost story. But you're wrong.

That night in the Burangie pub we slept like logs. After breakfast next morning Constable Fiddler called. He had already been out to see the wreckage of the Ferryman's Arms. The river was blocked and had flooded the whole valley. Mr Trivett, we now learned, was a pensioner who fossicked for gold up in the hills. He was in the hospital, chirpy as a cricket.

"We were sure he was the ghost who lived in the Ferryman!" said Fenella.

"Nobody House was supposed to be haunted all right," said the Constable, "though I didn't want to say so, straight out, in case you thought I was around the twist or something. But it wasn't haunted by an old-timer like Pop. The ghost was a boy of fourteen or so. Usually he was seen on the road before you reached the bridge."

Fenella and I just gulped. Dad said in a low kind of voice, "How . . . how did he become a ghost, if I may put it that way?"

So Constable Fiddler told us about the original Old Man Flood which, some forty years before, caused the Ferryman's Arms to fall into disuse. The boy had lived up in the hills on a farm. His people saw heavy water coming down the river, and they thought the Ferryman might be in danger. They tried to phone, but it was a bad line and they couldn't make themselves understood. So they sent the lad down with a message, but as he was crossing the bridge it collapsed and he was drowned.

I think it was our experience that night that changed Orrible to Fenella, an agreeable kind of person. Maybe it changed me, too. I wonder about things, though. Did we drive into the past that night, with the inn all lit up to welcome late travellers? And then the phone message which didn't quite get through but told us enough to frighten us and make us get out and save all our lives. Did that belong to the past, too? Because there WAS something queer about the time factor. Dad thought he was in the Nobody House for only a moment or so, but Fenella and I absolutely know it was much longer than that.

And that boy. He wasn't a bit like a ghost. In the car I touched his hand by accident, and it was as warm as mine. He was just – ordinary. It does make you wonder how many more of them there are about.

The Hook

Michael Rosen

It was a dark night and John was walking along an old country road. He was tired and the rain was beating down on his face. Where would he spend the night? He couldn't sleep out here in the rain, and the ground was sodden. On he walked. Again and again, he lifted his head into the rain and tried to make out the shape of a hut or a house. Nothing. But then, after what seemed hours, he noticed a dark hump by the side of the road that could be a house. And, indeed, the closer he walked, the more it took on the shape of a house. But at the same time, the nearer he stepped, the more strange and forbidding it seemed. High, dark, no lights.

He heard his feet on the stone path and after a moment's pause he pounded on the door with his hand. A light came on in the window above and then followed the sound of feet on the stairs. The bolts banged back, one at the top, one at the bottom, and

the key turned in the lock. When the door opened, John could make out a great slab of a man.

"What do you want?" he said.

"I seem to have lost my way," said John, "and I would be most obliged if you'd let me have a place to lie down for the night."

"Well, you've found the right place here," said the man. "This is an inn."

John felt a warm wave travel down his back and he saw himself passing through the luxuries of a hot bath, soft towels, hot soup, a roaring fire, a soft bed.

"Step right in," said the man.

John could have hugged him.

And indeed, it was just as he had imagined: the bath, the towels, the soup, the fire and the bed.

Just before he settled down for the night, John looked around the room. He caught sight of himself in the mirror, his eyes dark and tired. He draped his clothes over a chair and hung his old rucksack on a hook on the wall and fell asleep before he knew it.

A couple of hours later he woke up. The room was pitch black. He scarcely knew he had opened his eyes. He lay there for a moment wondering why he had woken up – then slowly he realized he could smell smoke. He sniffed the cold air. That was most definitely smoke. John lay in his bed staring into the blackness. Smoke ... smoke ... he said the word over in his mind not thinking what it really meant until quite suddenly it joined another word – fire? He felt gripped with a terror.

Where am I? Where is the fire? Above me, below me, alongside me? How will I get out? And yet, though his mind ran wild, his body lay still. He couldn't move. Then he heard the rushing of feet outside his room, muffled shouts, a cry in the distance. It was then that he realized his body was so overcome with tiredness from the day before that it wouldn't move until he told it to.

Move! And now the legs kicked the blankets off, the arms grabbed the clothes, the hands seized the door handle and the feet took him out of the door. Someone dashed past him in the passage and he saw flames curling out of a doorway. He turned and ran to the stairs.

But where there were stairs before was now a pool of white smoke. Right next to his ear a flaming beam roared down into the pool of smoke, followed by a sickening scream. He looked back and the flames that curled out of the doorway were now reaching towards him. He had no choice. Jump or be burned alive. But jump into what? John asked himself no more questions, covered his face with his shirt and leapt into the pool of white smoke.

He landed on a burning banister, jumped off before

it could burn him and, on looking up, saw a dark hole. Without knowing why, he jumped for it, dived into it, lunging through it. Only then did he realize how wise a move he had made. The dark hole was the night, visible for a brief moment when a door fell to the floor. John looked at himself. He was outside the inn, standing in the courtyard in his night-shirt, looking up at the blazing building.

A wall of flame stood between him and the room he had just leapt from. Upstairs was a furnace, sparks rising into the night air like fireworks. He turned away and ran, only now realizing what a horrible death he had just avoided. He ran down the road he had walked earlier that night. There must be another house near by, he thought, and he ran on faster than he had ever run before.

A house came into view. He ran to the door and slammed the knocker against it again and again.

He screamed out, "The inn's on fire. The inn down the road's on fire. People are dying. Help! Help!"

Someone stuck their head out of the window above him, "What's going on? What the devil do you think you're doing?"

"Can't you hear me?" shouted John. "The inn's on fire. People are dying. Get out of bed and help."

The voice above said, "Hold your horses, man. What are you talking about? There's no inn up the road, we're the only house this side of the moor till you get to the sea."

"For God's sake, believe me. I know what I'm saying, I was there, just now, I've just come from there. I was asleep . . . I was . . ."

His voice faded.

One way or another he managed to persuade the man of the house and his brother to come with him up the road. But no matter where they looked there was no inn, no fire, no smoke, no ashes. Nothing. Well, not exactly nothing.

Beside the road, in a place where an inn might once have stood, was an old ruin. By now it was dawn, the sky was growing lighter and they could see the old mossy stones lying in heaps, the broken walls leaning against trees as if looking for help.

John ran amongst them. He was beginning to feel bewildered and anxious. The layout of the rooms seemed the same as the inn. There was the back door, the little lobby, the back room, and yes, there were a few of the steps up to the first floor, which would mean – his eyes were flicking to and fro with the excitement of it now – which would mean that just up there, along that wall, yes, that would have been the room he had slept in. But it was impossible. This was the ruin of a house that must have been standing here over a hundred years ago.

And then he saw it. Something up on the wall that made his whole body freeze. There, next to the place where his bed might have been, was a hook. And on the hook was – his rucksack.

A Kind of Swan Song

Helen Cresswell

When I say that Lisa was someone special, right from the beginning, I expect that you will smile. *All* mothers think their children are special – and so they are, of course. In my case, Lisa was my only child, and so you will think that perhaps it is only natural that I should think her special. And when I tell you that my husband (who was a violinist with a well-known symphony orchestra) died when she was only a few months old, then you will quite understandably suspect me of exaggeration. I don't blame you. This is how it might seem.

But I must insist – Lisa *was* special. And perhaps it is partly because it is important to me that other people should realize this too, that I am now writing her story. It will not take long. She was only eight when she died.

The other reason I feel bound to tell her story is because I want you to know, as certainly as I now do myself, that death is not the end, not a full stop.

"Ah," I hear you say, "but she is *bound* to say that. She had no one in the world but her little daughter, and she died. Now she is trying to convince herself that death is not the end of everything. It's understandable, but she can't expect *us* to believe that!"

To this I simply reply – "Wait. Wait until you have heard my story. Then decide."

At birth, Lisa was special to Peter and myself in exactly the same way as any other baby born to loving parents. In our case, there was an extra dimension to our joy, because we knew already that in Peter's case it was to be short-lived. We knew that he had only a few months, at most, to savour the delights of parenthood. He had had to leave the orchestra several weeks before her birth. And so, for those first few months of Lisa's life Peter was as close to her as any father can be. He would sit with her for hours, studying her tiny, peaceful face as if he wanted to imprint it on his heart forever. In the early days, before he grew too weak, he would bathe her, change her, put her to bed.

And then he would play music to her, for hours on end. Not himself – he had sorrowfully put his violin away before her birth, but on tapes, and records. She would lie there kicking on the rug to the strains of Bach and Mozart, songs of Schubert and grand opera.

Sometimes I would laugh and say that I thought it all rather beyond the grasp of a baby, and that we should be playing her nursery rhymes instead. But he would say quite seriously, "That baby may not be able to talk, yet, but she can hear. She is listening, the whole time, trying to make a pattern of this strange new world she has entered. If what she hears is joyful, if she hears harmony, then all her life long she will seek out joy and harmony for herself. Believe me, Martha, I know that I am right."

Even at the time I acknowledged that what he said might be true. Now, I know that it was.

I don't want to give the impression by this that we were too serious about things, or that Lisa had a strange start in life. Like any young parents we romped and played with her, looked for ways of making her smile or, better still, laugh. And we sang nursery rhymes as well. But I honestly think that the times she loved best, the times when she seemed happiest, were when she was lying there listening to music – especially songs. There was a special peaceful, wondering look she seemed to wear when she heard a beautiful human voice singing great music.

I don't want to exaggerate this – it is how I

remember it, but then perhaps my memory of that time is not very reliable. It is a strange thing for a woman to watch her child blossom and at the same time her husband, the father, fading. Joy and sorrow could hardly be more poignantly interwoven.

Peter refused to let me grieve openly, and himself would show no sign of bitterness that he must soon leave us.

"I want there to be no shadows over her," he said. "Let her be shaped by music, not by sorrow."

Strangely, afterwards, when she was four or five, she would insist that she remembered Peter, though she could not really have done so.

"He was always smiling," she would say. And that

was certainly true, so far as she was concerned. If there were times when he allowed his smile to fade, it was never in her presence.

He died when she was just over eight months old – in time to see her crawling, but before she took her first steps.

"Promise you will keep playing her music," he said before he died. And of course I promised. And that was another strange thing.

In those unreal, nightmarish days after he died, Lisa grew pale and quiet. It was as if she, too, were mourning. Then, coming back into the house after the funeral, drained and weary, I was suddenly aware of the great silence and absence. It occurred to me that since Peter died, I had played no music. I went and put on a record – one of his favourites, from Haydn's *Creation*. As the pure, triumphant notes swelled about me, I lay back in a chair and surrendered myself to it. Then, beyond that marvellous music, I heard, in a pause, another music, another voice – Lisa's.

I hurried into the next room where she lay, as I thought, sleeping. Instead, she lay there wide-eyed – and round mouthed, too. Her whole tiny being seemed intent on the sounds that she was making with such seriousness, such concentration – Lisa was singing.

Very well – perhaps she was not. Perhaps she was simply cooing, crooning, as babies do. But to me, in my overwrought condition, it seemed that she was singing, herself joining in Haydn's great celebratory hymn. I remember that my tears, all at once released, splashed down on to her face, and that I gathered her up and took her with me, and she lay against me while we listened together.

Some children walk before they talk, some the other way round. Lisa, I swear, sang before she did either. I have the courage to say this, in the light of what came after. I did not merely imagine that Lisa was a child of music. She quite simply, and unarguably, was.

At first it was only I who knew it, and who could hardly believe it when I heard that infant voice playing with scales as other children play with bricks. (She did that, too. She was in every way exactly like all other children of her age. Only this was different – music ran in her veins.)

Then, as she grew older and we went to play-groups, others would remark on the purity and the pitch of her voice, and noticed that she had only to hear a song once to know it off by heart.

"She takes after her father," they all said.

It was true. But only I knew that she was composing music, as well as singing it. She would lie in bed after I had tucked her in for the night, her voice tracing its own melodies in the darkness. Sometimes even I, her own mother, would give a little shiver.

The word "genius" is not an easy one to come to terms with. Every mother, as I have said, believes her own child to be special. But I do not think that any mother is looking for genius. It is rather a frightening thing, for ordinary people. We admit that it exists – but at a great distance, and in other people (preferably long since dead!).

At two Lisa was picking out tunes on the piano; at three she was playing both piano and violin. But it was the singing that mattered, I knew that. I watched her grow and develop with a delight tinged with sadness. I knew even then that the days of our closeness were numbered. Soon the world would discover her, and then the music would no longer be our shared secret.

When she was only four photographs of her were beginning to appear in the papers, under headlines such as "Child Prodigy wins Premier Award at Festival" and "Little Lisa Triumphs Again".

I don't want you to think that she was in any way strange. She was exactly like every other little girl in most ways. She loved reading, roller-skating and using her computer. When she started school, her marks were average. It was only the music that set her apart.

When she was five all kinds of renowned people – professors and teachers of music – began to visit us. "Soon," I thought, "they will take her away from me."

They wanted me, even then, to send her away to a special school, where her gift could be nurtured.

"It doesn't need nurturing," I told them. "It is natural. It will flower of its own accord."

They went away again, but I knew that it would not be for long. I knew, too, that what I had told them was only partly true. *Any* gift needs the right nourishment, just as a rare and fragile plant.

Lisa herself began to grow away from me. Not in the things that mattered – the things between mother and daughter. In those things we were always close. We teased each other a lot, and sometimes, even then, it would seem as if she were older than I was.

"Dear goose mother!" she would say, if I forgot something, or made a mistake. It became her pet name for me.

At six they tried to take her away again, and again I resisted.

"It's too soon," I said. "She's too young. Leave her with me a little longer, then she can go."

This time, when they had gone, I thought I could sense a sadness in her, a disappointment. I thought perhaps that I was being selfish, over-possessive. And so when they came again, begging me, almost, to send her away, I gave in.

Her delight when she heard the news hurt me, and she must have seen this.

"I'll still be home in the holidays, dear goose mother," she told me. "Don't be sad, or you'll spoil it for me."

So I tried to look glad, for her sake. During those last few months together before she went away, I gathered her music together, to comfort me in her absence. Every song she composed I made her sing into a microphone so that I could record it. I recorded her playing the piano and the violin too, but it was the singing that mattered. We both knew that. When she sang, instrument and music were one, perfect and inviolable.

She was still only seven when she left for her new school. She was radiant. She was like a bride in beret and navy socks.

"No crying, goose mother," she told me. "We'll write to each other."

"And send me tapes," I said. "Please, Lisa. Don't let even a single song you make get away. Put it on tape. That way, we've got it forever."

She smiled then with a curious wisdom.

"It's *making* the song that matters," she said. "*Nothing* gets away – ever."

When she had gone, I *did* cry, as I knew I would, and I kept remembering those words. How could she *know*, I wondered, something that most people never learn in a lifetime?

I took a job – an interesting one, really – in a house belonging to the National Trust, and open to visitors. Even so, the first term dragged. Most evenings I would sit and listen to the tapes we had made that summer. And at weekends I'd go shopping – looking for little things to put in her stocking. Lisa still believed (at least, I think she did) in Father Christmas.

By mid-December she was home. For a day or so we were a little strange together, and then it was as though she had never been away. One evening, we turned on the television to see a programme of carols composed by children. It was a competition, and these were the winning entries. When it was over, Lisa said quietly, "Next year, goose mother, I shall make a carol!"

That was all. It was so slight a thing that, were it not for what followed, I doubt whether I should have remembered it. Lisa, after all, had been making songs almost all her life. What was more natural than that she should make a carol?

Christmas and the New Year came and went. This time, when she left for school, the wrench was not so painful. We can become in time accustomed to most things – even to the absence of those we love. It all seemed inevitable, and for me, it was also part of the promise I had made to Peter before he died.

Lisa's letters came every week – badly spelt, and full of the things she was doing, the music she was making. They were full, too, of the ordinary things – requests for clothes that were all the rage, for stamps to swap and posters for her room. That term passed, and the next. In the summer I took a cottage in the Lakes, and we spent most of the time walking and cycling. We were well on the way to establishing a pattern to our lives.

It was sometimes hard to remember that she was still only eight years old. And we never talked about what she would "do" when she was "grown up". Looking back, I think that this was because she was already what she was meant to be. She was all the time in a process of becoming, and this was all that was necessary. She knew it herself.

"It's *making* the song that matters," she had said, over a year ago.

Again I waved her off to the start of a new school year. This time the ache was not so bad. I even registered for evening classes in Italian, and went out occasionally with friends to the theatre, or for a meal. But Lisa still made the tapes, and I still played them, hour upon hour. Now, she was beginning to write her own words to the music. One day I received a cassette with a song called "Goose Mother" and I felt so happy and so honoured that I actually taped it again, on to another cassette, for fear that it might get lost or damaged. Even as I did so, I seemed to hear her saying, "It's *making* the song that matters". I smiled wryly.

"For you, perhaps," I thought. "But for the rest of us, who can only listen, it's the song itself that counts."

In November I was surprised by Lisa calling me on

the telephone. This she had done only once before – to inform me that she had chicken pox, but there was no need to worry, and proudly announce the number of spots she had.

"Listen," she said, "I've made a carol!"

"A carol?" I echoed.

"Remember – that competition we saw? And listen – Davey's going home, for the weekend, and I can go with him! So you and I can record it together – on our own piano!"

"Darling, that's wonderful!" I said. "But . . ."

"Look – his mother's coming to fetch us in the car. I'll be home Friday, at around six. Can't stop now – bye!"

That was all. It was Tuesday – three days to get used to the wonderful fact that Lisa was coming home. I had quite forgotten (how could I?) that during their first year children at the school were not allowed to go home during term-time, but that this rule was lifted after that.

I spent the interim pleasurably shopping for Lisa's favourite food (not a difficult task, this being mainly a variation on chicken) and bought a new duvet cover for her bedroom. By half past five on the Friday I was fidgeting in the kitchen – opening and re-opening the oven door to check on the degree of brownness of chicken and potatoes, wondering whether I should start thawing the chocolate mousse.

At quarter to six I remembered that I hadn't any fizzy lemonade – her favourite drink, and one not allowed at school. I hesitated.

"I'll write a note," I thought, "and pin it on the door. I'll only be five minutes."

Accordingly I wrote "Back in five minutes" and pinned it on the door and set off. There were no shops nearby. I took the car and made for the nearest late-night supermarket. The traffic was dense, irritatingly slow. I had forgotten what Friday night rush hours were like. At one point, I almost seized the opportunity to turn round and go home without the lemonade. But, I reflected, people rarely arrived on time, especially at the weekends. I carried on.

It was nearly quarter past six when I arrived back. In the space my own car had occupied only half an hour previously, was another. It was a police car. I drew alongside it, oblivious to the hooting behind me. Two figures, a policeman and a policewoman were standing on the steps up to the front door.

I wrenched open the door and got out. I was telling myself to keep calm. My knees were trembling.

"What – what is it?"

They turned. Their faces were young, worried, pitying.

"Mrs Viner?"

I nodded. "Perhaps we can . . .?"

I hardly remember what happened then exactly. Somehow I was inside, somehow I was sitting in my usual chair facing the fire and a voice was talking to me. It was a sympathetic voice, its owner reluctant to give me the news. "Motorway . . . wet surface . . . central reservation . . . lorry . . ." The words washed over me. What they were telling me was that Lisa was dead. She had been killed, along with her friend and his mother, on the motorway.

They were very kind. The young woman made me a cup of tea and switched off the oven. Before they left they stood looking at me uncertainly, at a loss. They didn't know what to say.

"Funny thing," said the policeman, "we'd been there on the steps ten minutes before you came."

I said nothing.

"Could've sworn there was someone in here," he went on. "Could hear someone singing – a kid, it sounded like."

"We wondered if the radio had been left on," the girl added.

"And now I come to think of it," he said, "the radio wasn't on. Or the telly. Funny, that . . ."

"Yes, funny," I said. "Thank you. Thank you both very much. I think – I think I want to be alone now."

They hesitated.

"Sure you'll be all right?"

"Sure."

They went. The door closed and I was alone. I sat there for I don't know how long. I was seeing Lisa, hearing her, trying to tell myself that I would never see or hear her again. I couldn't cry. I just sat, dry-eyed, remembering.

In the end, after a long dark age, I got up. Mechanically I began turning things off, locking up for the night. The front door, the back, check the oven – still containing the chicken and crisp potatoes – switch off lights, pull out the plug of the TV . . .

I stopped. All the lights but one were out. There, glowing in the darkness, were the red and green lights of the stereo deck and cassette recorder. There was a very faint hum. My mind was dense, confused. I had set up the system, that very afternoon, all ready to record the carol. The blank cassette was in place, I had carefully checked the sound levels. *And then I had switched it off.*

I remembered doing it. I had actually thought of the way Peter had always chided me for leaving things on – especially the cassette recorder. He had lectured me about the damage it might do.

I advanced towards the deck. Hesitantly, I pressed

the PLAY switch. There came only a faint hissing. Then, hardly knowing why I did so, I pressed REWIND. *The tape rewound.* It stopped with a click.

"But it was a new cassette," I thought. "Brand new."

I stood there for a long time in the dim remaining light. Then I pressed another key – PLAY.

The room filled with sound. A noise – Lisa's voice, pure and sweet, sang.

"On a far midnight,

Long, long ago . . ."

There was no accompaniment, no piano, just that young, miraculous voice, singing of that long-ago miracle that Christmas celebrates.

I stood dazed, listening. Then, when at last the carol ended, I heard – or thought I heard (it certainly was not there on the tape, afterwards) – "There, dear goose mother! I told you – it's *making* the song that matters!"

And I knew that this was her last present to me. It was not for her own sake, but for mine, that the carol was there, locked for all time, on tape.

I sent that tape to the contest. It won. The presenter said, "It is with great sadness that we have to tell you that Lisa, aged eight, died tragically in a car accident, just after she had recorded this carol for our concert. It was to be her swan song."

Only I knew that the carol had been recorded not before, but after the accident. Though perhaps it could, after all, be called a *kind* of swan song.

The Hitch-hiker on Blueberry Hill

Maeve Friel

itch-hiking is dangerous: you don't need me to tell you that. When I was a student, though, that wasn't the case. I used to regularly thumb the two hundred odd miles between my home town and the city where I went to university and nothing awful ever happened to me, nothing worse than getting bored and angry hanging around the outskirts of depressing provincial towns as smug drivers sped past me. It always seemed to be raining and the wheels of the passing cars flung dirty puddles of water over my clothes. I made up my mind then that once I had a car I would never turn a blind eye to hitch-hikers. But times change. You hear stories about drivers being mugged. You forget what it feels like to be sitting on a cold draughty road verge watching the traffic streaking past and getting less and less choosy about what you'll take. The novice hitch-hiker's fantasy of bowling alone in a Mercedes or open-top convertible is quickly abandoned – you'd take a ride on the back of a slurry tanker if you could just get to where you need to be.

On the night I want to tell you about, I was driving into the city on my own. It was a filthy night, with the rain coming down in sheets. There were no stars, or if there were, they were all blotted out by the dull orange glow of the city street lights. I was half listening to a play on the radio when I realized I must have taken the wrong exit at the Blueberry Hill roundabout and was once more heading out towards the airport, in precisely the opposite direction that I wanted. I swore at myself with annoyance, turned off the radio and hunched over the steering wheel, furious at having wasted so much time. The windscreen wipers swept backwards and forwards in an angry impatient rhythm. A huge lorry loomed out of the distance, bearing down on me with its head lamps on full. As it passed it threw a sheet of mucky water on my window so that I was almost blinded and swerved dangerously towards the middle of the road.

It was then that I saw the girl. She was running along on the opposite pavement, her head turned back to watch the oncoming traffic, one arm outstretched, thumbing a lift.

"What a night for hitching," I thought. And immediately afterwards thought how stupid she was to be hitching at that time of the evening with such dark clothes on.

A few minutes later, I reached the roundabout where I had gone wrong, drove right in a complete circle, counting off the exit roads, and eventually got back on to the correct route for the city centre, heading down Blueberry Hill. The rain, if anything, had got heavier. My headlamps soon picked out the girl again. She was still running along the side of the road, head twisted back to look at the traffic, thumb pointing upwards. As I approached she stopped running and looked directly at me. Our eyes met. It gave me a jolt, like that sense of déjà vu when you think, "But this has happened to me before." I certainly didn't know her – I was probably just remembering the many occasions I had looked at drivers with that same expression of pleading and desperation after a long day's hitching in the rain. I put my foot sharply down on the brake and pulled in to the verge. I had been travelling quite fast so the girl had to run a hundred yards or so to catch up. As she came near, I leant across and opened the passenger door for her to climb in but instead, she opened the back door and sat behind me. I shrugged, turned back and smiled at her and pulled the door shut again. She was probably just playing safe.

"City centre all right for you?" I asked.

"That would be terrific, thanks," she replied. "I'm sorry I'm getting your car so wet. I missed the bus into town and there isn't another for ages. My mum will be going crazy."

I glanced back at her in my rear-view mirror. She was younger than I had thought, just about fourteen, very pretty with wide grey eyes and long eyelashes. Her cheeks were streaked with smudges of black mascara which had run in the rain.

"I must look a sight," she said, laughing. She moved towards the middle of the seat so that she could look in the mirror. She rubbed at the mascara with long thin fingers, spreading the stains further, and made a funny face at herself. Then she scraped her hair back into a pony-tail and began to squeeze the water from it, totally absorbed in herself, humming tunelessly. She might have been sitting in the car with her own mother, safe and secure, instead of driving along on a winter's night with some stranger for company. I felt suddenly very apprehensive for her, alarmed by her complete innocence. She was too young to know how attractive she was and to understand that the world is a dangerous placed, full of wicked people. Very soon she would have to learn to be on guard, but for the moment she felt independent, unconcerned for her own safety. I was afraid for her but touched as well. I was glad that I had picked her up and not some weirdo.

"Do you live near the centre?" I asked.

"If only!" she laughed, throwing her hair over her shoulder. "No, we live right out by the old gravel pits – you know where I mean?"

I vaguely knew the area she meant. They had long ago flooded the old pits and turned what had once been an industrial wasteland into a nature reserve. "Yes, I think I do," I said. "Wasn't there something about it on the television some time ago? I expect

you're an expert on all the birds that have colonized it now?"

"Not really," she said, grinning. "I'm not that into birds myself."

"What are you into?" I asked.

"Just this and that. Going out with my friends. Having a laugh."

We had nearly arrived at the city centre. There were more traffic lights, all apparently programmed to turn red as I approached. I glanced at my watch. It was almost eleven o'clock. I had been looking forward to a gin and tonic with a friend of mine before going to bed but I was probably not going to make it.

"Tell me, where's the best place to leave you to catch your bus home?"

"Don't worry," said the girl. "Anywhere will be fine. I'll thumb the rest of the way now."

No, I thought to myself, that will not do. You're a children's writer. You'd never forgive yourself if anything happened to this young girl. I had visions of a hit-and-run, a body tossed into a gutter, ambulances and revolving blue lights, casualty wards, tearful mothers, plaster of Paris, crutches, bandages. My problem is I have a vivid imagination. Not vivid enough, as it happens.

"Let me drive you home," I said, turning around. "It's not far from where I'm going. Really." Goodbye to that gin and tonic. It would be midnight before I got to my friend's house and I had an early start the next morning.

"Would you? Oh, thanks a million." The girl was wreathed in smiles. She positively sparkled. "Mum will be so pleased when I get home."

We drove down the dual carriageway, past the flooded gravel pit with its resident swans and water-hens and tufted ducks invisible now in the night shadows. The girl was leaning on the back of my seat, giving me directions, right here, second left. I could smell the minty chewing-gum on her breath. We turned into a terrace of tall Victorian houses with steps leading up to the front door. I could see by the rows of doorbells that some had been divided into flats. Others were smarter, coming up in the world – no doubt their new owners had been tempted into the area by the views overlooking the newly created lake and the bird reserve. Cities are always full of these surprising little backwaters.

"Here," said the girl. "Stop here. The one with the yellow door."

I stopped, put on the hand-brake, released my seat belt and gratefully massaged the back of my neck which was acting up after my long drive, then realized something was wrong. I turned around. The girl was gone.

"Hey, stop kidding," I said. "What are you hiding for? Have you dropped something on the floor?"

There was no answer. I looked over into the space between the front and back seats. She was gone.

But she could not have gone. I had not heard the car door open or close. In any case she would not have gone without saying goodbye or thanking me. Would she? My heart began to thump. I was suddenly afraid for my own safety, all alone in an area I did not know, where no one knew me. Had I allowed myself to be drawn into some sort of trap? Was she lying in wait ready to mug me, the scheming little brat? I tried to remember if I had left my handbag on the back seat.

Slowly, carefully, I took the keys out of the ignition, hopped out of the car and pulled open the back door. The car was empty – as I had known it would be.

I looked up and down the street – nothing moved. It wasn't logical. She could not have disappeared as quickly as that. I glanced up at the house with the yellow door. The curtains upstairs and downstairs were all drawn but there was still a light burning in the hall. I boldly ran up the few steps and rang the front door-bell. I waited for at least a minute, listening to the silence of the house. I had almost decided to leave when I heard footsteps coming down the hall. A bolt was drawn back, then another. The door opened.

"Yes?" It was a woman, late thirties, very thin, attractive, with wide dark eyes. She was wearing a white towelling dressing-gown.

"I'm sorry I got you out of bed," I began, feeling truly foolish. "It's just that . . . I think I may have lost someone . . . Did a girl come in here a moment ago?"

"You too?" the woman said. "You had better come in. You're the fourth person this has happened to."

I allowed myself to be drawn into a pretty sitting-room on the left of the hallway. The woman turned on the lights and asked me to sit down on the sofa in front of the fireplace. There were still the remains of a log fire burning in the grate. On the mantelpiece was a selection of photographs in silver frames. A shiver ran down my spine. They were all pictures of the pretty hitch-hiker.

"That girl?" I said, pointing. "Did she come in?" My voice sounded quite wobbly.

"No," said the woman, sadly. "Today is the anniversary of my daughter's death. She died three years ago."

"Died?" I echoed.

The woman placed a glass in my hand. "Please sit down," she said, "and let me explain."

Her name was Rachel. She was thirteen when she

died. They had just moved to the house with the yellow door and Rachel was missing her friends from her old neighbourhood. She had sneaked off to the other side of town one Friday night without telling anyone where she was going. Afterwards, when the police were trying to piece the story together, various people had come forward to say that someone of her description had been spotted hitch-hiking on Blueberry Hill. The last person to see her did not come forward. Her body was discovered by police divers in the gravel pit near her home four days after her disappearance.

Since that night, three other drivers, middle-aged women like me, travelling alone, have picked up a girl at that spot and brought her home to her mother. Each has told the same story, each mentioned the minty chewing gum, the streaked mascara, the carefree happy manner. Each explained how Rachel had sat in the back seat, how she said she had missed the bus. Each remembered her saying, "Mum will be so pleased when I get home." Each woman felt she must take her home personally.

"It is as if," her mother told me, "my daughter is running and re-running the night she died, trying to reach home in safety."

"And you have never seen her?" I asked softly.

"No," said Rachel's mother, tears now springing to

her eyes. "All of you tell the same story, that she disappears as soon as the car stops in front of the house."

"Perhaps you should start again somewhere else?" I suggested.

"No," said Rachel's mother. "I will never leave in case some night a stranger brings me back my daughter and I am not here to answer her knock."

We shook hands. Her fingers were long and thin, like her daughter's, but with nails bitten back to the quick.

Hands are so expressive. Just think how much they can tell us without a word being spoken. A hand outstretched, palm upwards, begging. A raised arm waving goodbye. A raised fist, angrily punching the air. Fingers of hands knotted together in prayer. Thumbs up, thumbs down. A clenched fist, one thumb pointing downwards like an ancient Roman casting a disappointing gladiator to the lions. And that symbol of more modern times: one arm outstretched, fingers closed, one thumb raised. That simple gesture led to Rachel's murder.

I got back in to my car but sat for a few minutes, too dazed and shaken to drive off. As my eyes grew accustomed to the light, I could make out opposite the house the outline of the lake that had become Rachel's watery grave. I shuddered and turned around to put on my seat belt. The back of my seat still bore the damp traces where she had leant, not half an hour before, giving me the instructions to take her home.

When I visit the city now, I take a different route into the centre. I could not bear the pain of seeing that slender running figure, the hitch-hiking ghost of Blueberry Hill.

ACKNOWLEDGEMENTS

The publishers wish to thank the following for permission to reproduce copyright material:

Redvers Brandling: "Mayday!" reproduced by permission of the author.

Ann Carroll: "The Mirror" by Ann Carroll from *Chiller*; first published by Poolbeg Press 1995 and reproduced by permission of the author.

Ruth Park: "Somebody Lives in the Nobody House" by Ruth Park; reproduced by permission of Curtis Brown (Aust) Pty Ltd on behalf of Kemalde Pty Ltd.

Vivien Alcock: "Siren Song" from *Ghostly Companions* by Vivien Alcock, copyright © 1984 Vivien Alcock; first published by Methuen Children's Books and Mammoth 1984, pp. 1–18 and reproduced by permission of Egmont Children's Books.

Annie Dalton: "The Coming of the Wolf" from *Love Them, Hate Them* by Annie Dalton, copyright © 1991 Annie Dalton; published by Methuen Children's Books 1991, pp. 31–46 and reproduced by permission of Egmont Children's Books.

Helen Cresswell: "A Kind of Swan Song" by Helen Cresswell, copyright © 1984 Helen Cresswell; reproduced by permission of AM Heath & Company Ltd on behalf of the author.

Michael Morpurgo: "The Giant's Necklace" by Michael Morpurgo from *The Puffin Book of Ghosts*; reproduced by permission of David Higham Associates on behalf of the author.

Alison Prince: "Can't Help Laughing" by Alison Prince; reproduced by permission of Jennifer Luithlen Agency on behalf of the author.

Sorche Nic Leodhas: "The Man Who Didn't Believe in Ghosts" from *Gaelic Ghosts* by Sorche Nic Leodhas, Holt Rinehart and Winston, Inc. Copyright © 1964 Leclaire G. Alger; reproduced by permission of McIntosh and Otis, Inc.

Michael Rosen: "The Hook" by Michael Rosen, copyright © 1992 Michael Rosen from *The Oxford Book of Children's Stories* published by Walker Books and reproduced with the permission of Peters Fraser & Dunlop Ltd.

Maeve Friel: "The Hitch-hiker on Blueberry Hill" by Maeve Friel from *Chiller*, copyright © 1995 Maeve Friel; published by Poolpeg Press and reproduced with the permission of Ed Victor Ltd.

ACKNOWLEDGEMENTS

Peter Dickinson: "The Spring" from *Touch and Go* by Peter Dickinson, published by Macmillan Children's Books 1999; reproduced by permission of AP Watt Ltd on behalf of the author.

Tony Richards: "Someone Drowned" by Tony Richards; reproduced by permission of the author.

Terry Tapp: "The Green Ghost" by Terry Tapp; reproduced by permission of the author.

Margaret Biggs: "The King Stone" by Margaret Biggs; reproduced by permission of the author.

Every effort has been made to trace the copyright holders but where this has not been possible or where any error has been made the publishers will be pleased to make the necessary arrangement at the first opportunity.